Darwin's
DRAGONS

A MESSAGE FROM CHICKEN HOUSE

I've always been fascinated by those great natural discoveries from the past: the exotic animals from strange parts of the world, the secrets of the evolution of our own species *and others*. What if there was more to tell, *a lot more to tell*? Well – maybe there is! Lindsay Galvin imagines a dazzling secret, revealed in the pages of this stonking adventure – AND IT'S A CRACKER!

BARRY CUNNINGHAM
Publisher
Chicken House

Darwin's DRAGONS

LINDSAY GALVIN

2 PALMER STREET, FROME,
SOMERSET BA11 1DS
WWW.CHICKENHOUSEBOOKS.COM

Text © Lindsay Galvin 2020
Cover and interior illustration © Gordy Wright 2020

First published in Great Britain in 2020
Chicken House
2 Palmer Street
Frome, Somerset BA11 1DS
United Kingdom
www.chickenhousebooks.com

Lindsay Galvin has asserted her right under the Copyright, Designs and
Patents Act 1988 to be identified as the author of this work.

Cover and interior design by Steve Wells
Typeset by Dorchester Typesetting Group Ltd
Printed and bound in Great Britain by CPI Group (UK) Ltd, Croydon CR0 4YY

The paper used in this Chicken House book is made
from wood grown in sustainable forests.

5 7 9 10 8 6 4

British Library Cataloguing in Publication data available.

PB ISBN 978-1-912626-46-5
eISBN 978-1-913322-15-1

For Bill, with love.

Also by Lindsay Galvin

The Secret Deep

The natural history of these islands is eminently curious, and well deserves attention.

CHARLES DARWIN,
THE VOYAGE OF THE BEAGLE

Bricky
*brave, fearless, adroit – after the manner
of a brick: 'What a bricky girl she is.'
(See 'Plucky', 'Cheeky'.)*

JAMES REDDING WARE,
*PASSING ENGLISH OF THE
VICTORIAN ERA: A DICTIONARY OF
HETERODOX ENGLISH, SLANG AND PHRASE*

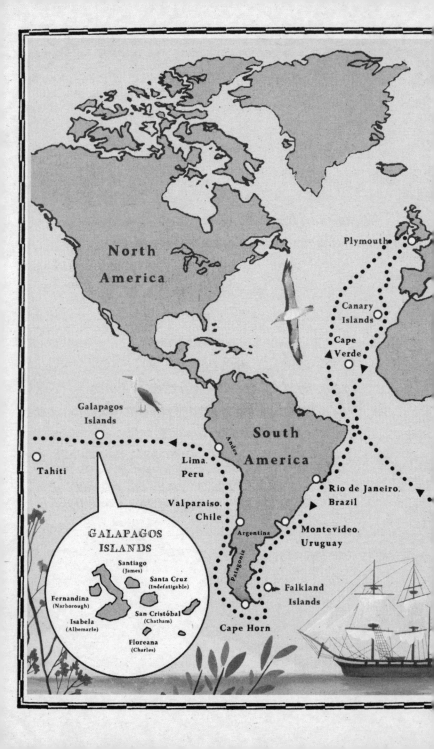

North America

South America

Plymouth

Canary Islands

Cape Verde

Galapagos Islands

Tahiti

Lima. Peru

Valparaiso. Chile

Argentina

Andes

Patagonia

Cape Horn

Rio de Janeiro. Brazil

Montevideo. Uruguay

Falkland Islands

GALAPAGOS ISLANDS

Santiago (James)

Santa Cruz (Indefatigable)

Fernandina (Narborough)

San Cristóbal (Chatham)

Isabela (Albemarle)

Floreana (Charles)

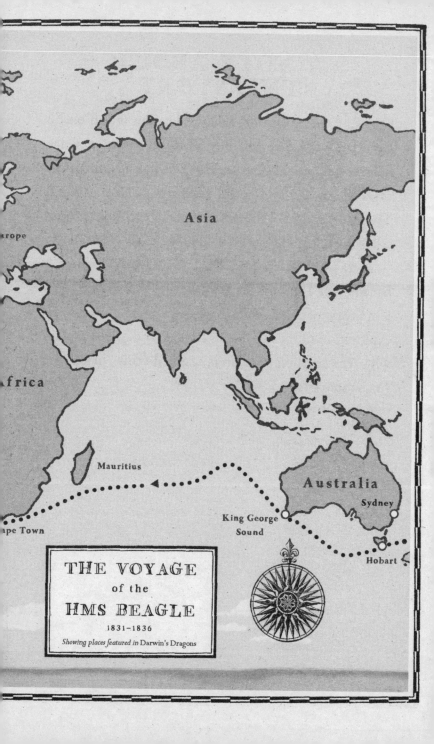

Europe

Asia

Africa

Australia

Mauritius

Sydney

King George
Sound

Cape Town

Hobart

THE VOYAGE
of the
HMS BEAGLE
1831–1836
Showing places featured in Darwin's Dragons

A NOTE ABOUT THIS STORY

On 27th December 1831 Charles Darwin set off on his legendary voyage aboard HMS *Beagle*. After five years, he returned to England with new and revolutionary ideas about the wonderful creatures he had studied. These ideas formed the basis of one of the most famous scientific books ever written, *On the Origin of Species*.

A cabin boy and fiddler called Syms Covington became Mr Darwin's assistant during the voyage. This is a story of what *could* have happened during their exploration of the Galapagos Islands, and might explain why the earliest explorers named this place the Enchanted Isles . . .

PART ONE

Narborough Island presents a more rough and horrid aspect than any other; the lavas are generally as naked as when they poured forth.

CHARLES DARWIN, *THE VOYAGE OF THE BEAGLE*,
30TH SEPTEMBER 1835

CHAPTER ONE

September 1835
Albemarle Island, Galapagos

Mr Darwin crouched in front of a giant tortoise, notebook in hand. His home-made magnifying eyeglass, which the sailors of the *Beagle* all made fun of, gave him the look of a studious buccaneer.

'See how the shell is completely domed, Covington,' he said. 'It means they can't raise their necks at all.'

'Reckon they don't need to, sir,' I said, watching the tortoises chewing. 'There's a lot of grass growing here, so they're always looking down at the ground anyhow.'

Mr Darwin's eyebrows shot up and he grinned. 'An interesting observation. Could the shell design force this behaviour, or could it be the other way around?'

I didn't know the answer to that but felt my cheeks warm in the glow of his approval. When our voyage began four years ago, I was Ship's Fiddler and Cabin Boy, but for the last two and a half years I'd been assisting Mr Darwin, making use of my letters, like my da would have wanted. I liked to think I'd picked up some of his way of thinking too.

'I wonder if it would be difficult to ride on such a shell,' I said idly, then kicked myself. That wasn't the kind of thing Mr Darwin wanted to hear from his assistant!

'Well ready yourself then,' said Mr Darwin, and to my surprise he clambered aboard one of the giant tortoises, perching on top of its shell. 'What are you waiting for?'

The ancient animal stretched out its long crusty neck and hissed at the unexpected weight, then took a ponderous step. Mr Darwin just managed to catch his balance. His laugh rang out, much clearer and louder than his voice, and he slapped his thigh.

This was more like it. The master might be awful clever and mostly serious but he was only a young man himself, and I loved those rare moments he was game for a lark. We'd been measuring tortoise shells all day and a break was more than welcome.

I eyed up the tortoises and chose a smaller one that seemed to be fast asleep, its head tucked into its wrinkled neck like an acorn in its cap. I scrambled on to its back. It wasn't as easy as Mr Darwin made it look. My master was tall and sometimes stooped. He had a way of swinging his arms when he walked, but wasn't nearly as clumsy as he looked. My knees slipped on the mottled shell, but I finally managed to settle my behind in the centre. When the tortoise started to move, I felt as though I was back on the *Beagle* sailing around the stormy waters of the Cape Horn.

Mr Darwin's tortoise was heading across the lava field but mine stopped and dipped to munch some grass, nearly tipping me off.

'You've chosen a donkey, Covington, but mine is a noble steed!' called Mr Darwin.

I laughed out loud as he waved his hat in the air. If only Da could see me now.

A shadow darted over me and I looked up. Two magnificent frigate birds swooped on the air currents, massive black wings almost as sharply pointed as their beaks and tails. Their red throats flashed.

Mr Darwin stared upwards too. 'Looks like some weather coming in, Covington . . .'

I could see it too. The sky was suddenly the colour of

a bruise and the air smelt of copper pennies.

The young sir hopped down from the tortoise. 'Did you pack the specimens well?' His voice was serious once more.

'I did, sir,' I replied, and slithered down myself. My tortoise had tucked its head back in. I pulled up some grass which it took from my offered hand with a beaky, toothless mouth. I liked the tortoises, there seemed to be a lot of thinking going on behind those old black eyes.

'Make haste then, boy. Let's get them back to the barrels,' said Mr Darwin.

The casks of wine would preserve the specimens we'd collected until we landed at a port where they would be sent all the way back to Mr Darwin's colleagues in Cambridge.

A fat spot of rain hit my arm and a gust of wind nearly separated me from my hat. The weather changed rapidly in this part of the world – we always had to be ready for it, and Mr Darwin's blue-grey eyes looked dark beneath his frown. I shouldered our knapsacks and stowed the logbook in my satchel. Mr Darwin's eyeglass had been discarded on a boulder, and I slipped it inside my fiddle case, then thumbed some wax around the seals to keep out the water. I'd brought my fiddle as an experiment to see the effect of music on wildlife, but there'd been no time to play in the end. Mr Darwin wasn't partial to the old instrument, he called it Scratch and the name stuck.

The spatters of warm rain turned into a downpour, and we hurried across the black lava plain towards the shore where the rowboat waited.

'Watch your step here, Syms,' said Mr Darwin, and I nodded. Beneath the lava plain were tunnels, which had once been underground rivers of molten lava, and there were dangerous holes near the surface.

Mr Darwin said these islands looked like the infernal regions – which to the likes of you and me, means hell. The five volcanoes of Albemarle lined up behind us, and ahead, purple-grey clouds the shape of cauliflowers had piled behind the silhouette of the *Beagle,* which was anchored out at sea.

One of the sailors, Robbins, met us at the shore in a bit of a lather, which wasn't like him at all. 'You've seen the storm then, sir?'

Mr Darwin nodded. 'Let's get back to the ship. All haste.'

Robbins took Mr Darwin's equipment and made giant strides through the bright green seaweed that covered the black rocks. We tramped straight in to the sea, wading out to the rowboat which was held steady in the surf by the other seaman, Tanner. I helped my master in first, then scrambled in myself. It had been minutes since our tortoise ride, but the *Beagle* was now near invisible through the rain, and the sea was dark and spiked. Robbins pushed off from the shore and waded through the surf, then leapt in behind us.

'Hold tight, lad. Mr Darwin.'

The two men began to row, muscles cording at their necks, as the swell of the sea rose and rain pelted us like stones thrown by a furious beast.

CHAPTER TWO

Lightning split the dark clouds above us and thunder shook my bones. From the first lurch of the rowboat, Mr Darwin's face turned the colour of ship's porridge, as it always did in any sort of swell. But as we pitched and rolled our way towards the *Beagle*, it was Robbins' stony face that scared me. He and Tanner were rowing with all their strength, but the waves were rising, the wind sharper than the bosun's whip, and it was hard to say if we were any closer to the ship.

I bailed rainwater from the bottom of the boat, but it poured in almost as fast as I could throw it out. I slid Scratch round to my back, glad I had sealed the case with wax. Each wave was a galloping hillock of water for us to climb and it seemed impossible we were still afloat, but the sailors rowed on and I tried to tell myself that it was harder to sink a boat than it looked.

Mr Darwin's linen shirt was plastered to his skin, his face as white as the foaming waves. He reached out to me, then scrambled across the bench and threw himself to the side of the boat to void his guts. He clung to the edge, his back heaving, and I moved over to help – but just as I did, we climbed a mountain of a wave and the master pitched forward, his hands slipping. Before I even had time to call out, he flipped over . . . into the sea.

'Man overboard!' Robbins yelled.

I snatched up the rope curled in the bottom of the rowboat, coiling it round my hand. Then another shout as I threw the other end of the rope behind me.

I leapt into the raging sea after my master.

The waves hauled me under and then threw me up, gasping, and I realized too late that I was a raw cove because I'd likely not be able to save myself, let alone Mr Darwin.

'Robbins!' I yelled. 'Robbins!' I felt the fiddle case rise at my back, still strapped tight across my chest. Everything was a blur of grey and white – was this the end? – then the line pulled taut in my hand. I collected my senses and kicked hard, trying to make out the silhouette of Robbins and the boat. And there . . . Mr Darwin's white shirt!

He wasn't lost, not yet. We had a chance. I must not let go.

Both our lives depended upon it.

I struck out with my free hand. Mr Darwin spotted me and floundered in my direction, tossed on the chop and foam like a cork, until by some force of luck, the swell clashed us into each other. I clung to him fiercely with my legs, and we were dragged under. We whirled and tumbled underwater before being flung to the surface again. By some miracle we were still together.

'Hold on to the rope, sir!' I shouted. He didn't seem to hear me. His eyes were almost closed and he hadn't so much as coughed since the last ducking. I held us both to the rope with one hand and slapped his waxy cheek, hard.

'The rope, sir! Mr Darwin!'

His eyes opened, but they were wide and glazed. I couldn't hold on to him for much longer.

'Charles Darwin!' I yelled in his face with all my strength. The master seemed to awaken then, spluttering out water, and his eyes sprung to life and met mine. He reached out and I snatched his hand and wrapped his stiff fingers around the rope, then his other hand next to it. I jerked hard and Robbins tugged back, then we were being hauled one way but the sea was sucking at us the other, trying to keep us for itself. But we were moving. All we had to do was hold on, and we'd make it.

The next whitecap battered me sideways and one of my hands was torn from the rope. Mr Darwin's feet crashed into my shoulder and then my other hand was slipping, slipping, and even when I gritted my teeth and crushed my fist tight, I couldn't keep hold. The sea wrenched the line from my hand and I was tumbled deep.

I spun until my lungs burnt, in an airless world of churning froth, and when I finally surfaced, gasping, neither Mr Darwin, the rope, the rowboat nor the *Beagle* were anywhere in sight.

CHAPTER THREE

The rain was like Noah's flood all over again; the sky matched the brutal slate grey of the sea, and flickered as though the clouds were giant flints clashing against each other. I was sure every new swell would be the one to finish me off, as I tumbled underwater over and over, unable to tell up from down. Memories flashed . . . taking me back where my mind hadn't been in years . . . to the day after they buried young Kitty Jenkins, who'd drowned in the Old River Bedford. Da had made me go down the pond with him.

Brown water in my eyes, in my mouth, sucking me down. I flailed, panicked, sinking, hearing nothing but the roar of the bubbles until Da's voice cut through muffled and distant.

'Kick, Syms! Kick hard!'

I booted the water with all my might and burst free coughing and sobbing. Strong hands grasped both of my upper arms.

'Now you can swim, boy. And that's what you do, you swim, and you never give up.'

I smashed through the surface, heaving in coughing breaths and hoped my da was looking down and feeling awful pleased that his son had legs that knew how to kick back.

How I wished I could catch a glimpse of the rowboat – for all I knew, it had been overturned and all on board lost . . . no. I didn't even know if Mr Darwin could swim, but many of the sailors could not. I had to trust, I *had* to believe, that my master had kept hold of the rope, that Robbins had hauled him in.

Over and over, I made it back to the surface like a bleeding boxer who didn't know when to quit. At last, at long last, the waters began to churn from below as well as above, and I felt jagged rocks beneath me. I fought to stay upright in the bubbling foam and could just see land ahead of me. Through my blurry salt stung eyes, it seemed no more than a great looming lump of black rock, but it might have been heaven itself, I was that pleased to see it.

I hauled myself up on to the rocks, out of the hungry sea, then scuffed my knees and hands as I dodged iguanas – the sea lizards which sprawled over the rocks on every Galapagos island, like wet rags on washday. One lifted its head and snorted out water from the nostrils in its craggy snub face, but the others gave me barely a glance. The *Beagle*'s commander, Captain Fitzroy had called them 'imps of darkness', but they weren't in the least impish in their nature.

I finally stood tall, battered by rain and trembling all over, and let myself believe I'd survived. I was scraped and bleeding, but the cuts weren't deep. My legs were wobbly, but I could walk. I had only one boot, but nearly all my senses. I had lost my master, my ship and even my fiddle, but I was alive.

Where was I?

The iguanas told me this was still the Galapagos at least. Ahead was one almighty summit, a bigger volcano than any I'd seen. Some of the islands had thick forests covering the higher ground, but the plains of black volcanic rock leading up to this one sprouted greenery as sparse as the feathers on a vulture's head. I hadn't been here before, I felt sure of it.

I crouched, hugging my knees, and tried to think. We'd been on the west coast of Albemarle this morning, but with the gusts of the storm I had no way of knowing which direction I'd been washed. I tried to picture the map of the archipelago, but my mind was whirling. I could have hit one of the other shores of Albemarle or been washed up on another island entirely. This place seemed by far the most wild and godforsaken of the Galapagos islands we had visited, and the driving rain was making it even less welcoming.

The relief I'd felt at being washed ashore was fading fast.

CHAPTER FOUR

I crouched on the black rocks, shivering – with fear and shock as much as cold – until my teeth chattered.

I pictured Mr Darwin's face when I last saw him – pale as a ghost, gripping the rope, terror widening his eyes. If only I'd got to him before he fell overboard . . . I should have seen it coming. Even if my master was hauled back and the rowboat made it – could the *Beagle* itself have been wrecked in the storm?

What if my master were to lose his life so young and only part way through his voyage? All his observations and measurements, all his ideas lost . . .

I put my hand to my chest and waited for my thumping

heart to slow. Letting my thoughts run this way would do no good at all. When my da was teaching me the fiddle, he'd say, 'If you hit a duff note, son, breathe. Walk that breath all the way upstairs to the attic, then right the way back down to the cellar. Not too fast mind, step by step. Breathe, and pretend like it's the best performance of your life. You keep right on playing and stay bricky.'

That's what I had to do now. I pulled in a breath slowly, step by step and back out again, and felt calmer. I uncurled and stood up straight.

Stay bricky.

Mr Darwin *was* alive, he would make it back to the *Beagle* and then he would search for me. Robbins too. Captain Fitzroy would figure out the wind direction and speed, and make calculations with the maps and his fancy navigation equipment to work out where I was likely to have ended up. I just needed to stay calm and survive until they arrived.

I forced myself to look around me and concentrate hard on what I saw. As Mr Darwin said on the first day he took me as his own servant, 'You will learn to observe and adapt, Covington. Open eyes lead to an open mind.'

I'd prepared enough expeditions to know what was needed, but all of them had been well planned and provisioned. Maudlin thoughts of thick canvas tents I didn't have weren't going to help me find water, and I now remembered that most of the Galapagos islands had no fresh water supply. Suddenly the driving rain went from being my enemy to my closest friend. I raised my face to the sky and let the rain tumble into my mouth until my neck cricked but my belly was tight.

It wasn't easy to get a sense of the time in the endless grey, but a patch of cloud glowed lighter than the rest and I guessed it was afternoon; might be time to find shelter before dark.

I struggled to my feet and began to stumble inland towards the dots of greenery in the direction of the volcano. Anything would be better than the bare rock I was currently surrounded by.

A tremendous screech sent my hands clinging to my ears. The sound jangled through my bones and I stumbled forward on to my hands and knees.

What the blazes?

A shadow swept over, blocking the rain, beating me with gusts of new wind. I covered my head as it passed, a second sickening shriek pounding my ears. What on God's earth could make such a racket? A bird? The frigate birds and albatross were big, but . . .

I staggered back to my feet, searching the sky before being punched forward, something gripping me from shoulder to leg. I was plucked from the ground, as an owl might snatch a mouse, and swept up, unbelievably, into the air.

CHAPTER FIVE

The rocks I had been walking upon seconds ago were left far below as I was swept higher and higher, face down and carried side on, the wind whistling in my ears and watering my eyes. Could this be all in my own mind? Was I off my chump? Sent into a flight of fancy by my ordeal at sea? I kicked at the air, my arms pinned tight to my sides in the grip that held my whole torso captive. I twisted and writhed, trying to get free, before realizing that this may not be a good idea at such a great height . . .

I tried to slow my ragged breaths, taking them up the stairs and down, and forced my legs to hang limp.

I looked down to see what imprisoned me. Colossal claws, as long as my forearm, attached to scaled bronze toes. They circled me from my chest to the top of my legs.

And these monstrous claws were all that stopped me from dropping to my death on the rocks below.

I was prey in the clutches of a flying predator. A bird, a beast – I couldn't tell.

I heard myself make a strangled sound, half sob, half feverish laugh. We were gaining height, and through my streaming eyes I saw we were heading out to sea. I kicked out again in terror, I couldn't help myself. My boot fell from my foot and spun through the air, hitting the rock below with a bounce. My skull would *not* bounce.

Stay bricky.

I gripped tight, as jolts passed through the beast's claws in time with the flap of its wings, which sounded like the snap and creak of a ship's sails. We were now over the sea. If I was dropped, would I have some chance or would the height make the sea as hard as rock?

A yelp was snatched from my mouth as my captor dived like an arrow, so fast all was a blur and the wind screeched in my ears . . . then the claws opened, and I was released.

Empty air was all that held me.

I tumbled head over foot, kicking and flailing at nothing, and hit the water so hard I thought the beast had dropped me on the rock after all, like a bird drops a mussel to break the shell. I never thought I would be pleased to be back in the sea, but when it washed around me, I felt a gush of relief. I kicked with all I had and swam to the surface, where I took in a lungful of water as a wave slapped me. I thanked the Lord over and over for the miracle that I was not yet dead.

Body aching, I struck out for shore and crawled on to the black rocks once again, coughing and sucking in heaving breaths before flipping to lie on my back among the uninterested iguanas, so I could scan the sky for the beast. No sign. *What was it?* The wind had dropped to nothing and it had stopped raining, an island storm that ended as suddenly as it started. If only Mr Darwin and I had waited it out on Albemarle . . .

I gazed up to see a huge mass hurtling towards me. The beast had returned. Silhouetted against the grey of the sky, I couldn't make out any details, but its wings were as big as the *Beagle*'s sails and strangely angular. It was coming for me again. I scrambled to my feet, but it swooped too fast for me to even attempt to run. I saw that its head was shaped like no bird I had ever—

I was grasped once more in those impossible claws and plucked from the rocks. This time I did not hold still, but squirmed and kicked, yelling all the while. It dropped me quickly, from less of a height but further out to sea.

The next time I crawled out of the sea, it didn't even wait for me to drag myself ashore but tweaked me right out from the breaking waves.

CHAPTER SIX

I was swept into the air at a sharp incline and quickly dropped over the sea again. This time I did not fight as I fell, and landed easier. The sky beast circled above and I stopped short of the shore, beyond the white water. I needed to do something different, I couldn't be grabbed and dropped over and over; it would eventually kill me. There – seaweed and driftwood were tangled together in a floating mass. I ducked under and surfaced in the centre of it, a wig of slimy kelp fronds perched on my head. In this camouflage, I floated. I had nothing left but my life, and I wasn't about to let that go. My mind raced as I peered upwards through the weed at the empty sky.

Unless it liked its food pickled in salt water, the creature might *not* intend to eat me after all. Exhausted, I swam very slowly sideways along the shore, behind the breakers, hauling my disguise with me like a hermit crab in its shell.

I waited . . . and just as I thought it had truly gone, it returned, circling high above, a dart of menace waiting to strike again. But what was it doing with me? I was unharmed.

'You could easily kill me,' I muttered, 'but you haven't, have you? You've bruised me something awful, but not even pierced the skin. Are you toying with me, like a cat with a mouse? Or is me being on your island making you as mad as hops? Cos I hardly have much choice, do I?'

Speaking out loud helped me get my thoughts running again. All very well Mr Darwin's 'open eyes, open mind', but I could make no sense of what business this giant beast had with me. I peered through the seaweed to see it hovering high, over the place it had last dropped me. It seemed like my disguise was holding up.

Its silhouette really was mighty strange. It had a long tail, like a snake, and four legs ending in those huge claws, like a reptile. Its wings were more like a bat than a bird. It banked and swooped scanning the shoreline for me. I ducked lower in my seaweed nest so only my eyes and nose were above water.

Giant tortoises were one thing, but I didn't know of any living thing *close* to this size. I might be only a cabin boy and fiddler, taught my letters and music by my own da and then the Dame School in the churchyard, but now I was Mr Darwin's servant, and I had learnt a lot about the world's creatures on this voyage. My mind sprang to years earlier, to the giant bones I had helped Mr Darwin dig from the cliffs in Punta Alta, Argentina. He'd explained that these bones were the ancient skeletons of animals that no longer existed, but I had not truly believed him until I helped strap a skull almost as big as I was to the back of a cart. I remember thinking that miracles like that could only be found in such a wild and distant place.

Well . . . Galapagos was as wild and distant as it was possible to be.

Could this thing, swooping in huge circles above, be a living example of one of those fossils? As I bobbed there, praying I wouldn't be discovered, it was the only explanation I had.

I forced myself to stay in the water long after the flying predator had disappeared inland towards the smoking summit of the volcano.

I had once heard Captain Fitzroy and Mr Darwin talk about how, back in 1525, a Spanish priest had been blown off course in the Galapagos – a bit like me – and had named the islands after the twitchy currents and the mysterious fogs: *Las Islas Encantadas*.

The Enchanted Islands.

If a colossal sky beast needed a secret home, the Galapagos was the place for it.

PART TWO

*These islands appear paradises for
the whole family of Reptiles.*

CHARLES DARWIN, *BEAGLE DIARY*
17TH SEPTEMBER 1835

CHAPTER SEVEN

When the sun disappeared, I finally dared to untangle myself from my seaweed camouflage and haul myself ashore once again. The wind had died and the moon was half full, with scraps of silver clouds crossing it wearily. I couldn't bear the thought of being seized by the sky beast again and dropped out to sea, this time in the dark. My lips were cracked from saltwater, my ears were ringing, my fingertips were the texture of tree bark.

I'd now lost both boots, but I was in one piece.

I stumbled across the rocks, shaking warmth back into my arms. Where I'd swum further along the shoreline, there were fewer iguanas. Instead there were scuttling red Sally Lightfoot crabs covering the rocks like a moving rag rug. The sound as they moved, strangely reminded me of my Sunday School teacher's clicks of disapproval: *tut, tut, tut*. I needed shelter. I crouched for a moment, scanning above for any sign of the sky beast either inland or out to sea. I was safe for now. Then I spotted something rolling in the surf. I knew that shape...

I staggered back into the waves, scooped up that battered old fiddle case – still closed, with its wax seal unbroken – and hugged it to my chest. In that moment I could not have been happier if I had found a knife, fire flints or anything else I so dearly needed, because now I was not completely alone.

Mr Darwin might not be awful keen on my tunes himself, but sailors love a shanty, which was how I'd ended up on board the *Beagle* in the first place. It wasn't the most tuneful of instruments, the young sir was right about that, but it had been my da's.

'If you can survive, Scratch, then I can too,' I whispered. There was a hitch in my voice because despite what the fiddle meant to me, I knew it must surely be ruined. Still, best be grateful for what I'd got.

I stumbled from the surf. When the clouds fluttered across the moon it was frightful dark. I imagined the others about the ship – mending ropes, smoking their pipes. They would surely miss my jigs and the hymns would be very mean without my accompaniment. But would they miss them enough to come and look for me? I had to believe they would. I'd build a fire, make a signal. Mr Darwin would have them row here as soon as the weather allowed.

If the master was alive.

Of course he was alive. They were all safe aboard the *Beagle* by now.

I remembered the gale that had hit the *Beagle* two years before, when we were rounding Cape Horn, the southernmost point of Chile. The ship had been hit beam on – directly in the side – and had nearly tipped right over, so half the deck was beneath water. For a teetering moment, all hands must have thought as I had, that we were lost, yet she had rolled upright again and the sea had poured back out through her ports. I smiled at the thought. The *Beagle* would easily ride out a common squall.

I picked up my pace as I hit scrubby grass – much more comfortable walking for my bare feet. The sky was still clear, although looking upwards made my heart race, expecting another attack.

In the far distance, the volcano was capped with a red glow; a cloud of smoke, lit from below. The volcano was active! Mr Darwin had always said how much he would like to witness an eruption. Well he could keep it, and good luck to him, because it was the last thing I needed right now. I gripped Scratch tighter to my chest and strode on. If ever a time were right for a fit of the vapours, this was not it. *Stay bricky*.

I found a cactus. I didn't know the name of it, but it was one of the taller types with a central trunk and then a branch either side at the top. It looked like the captain's brass candelabra, which I'd seen on his table when serving Sunday dinner for the officers. I sat beneath it, even though it would barely disguise me from above and the spikes meant I couldn't even lean against it. But it was better than sitting in the open, and my legs felt like a pair of jellied eels, they were that exhausted. I laid the fiddle case over my knees. It didn't slosh with water when I tipped it. I couldn't bear to feel hopeful, nor to see Scratch's ruin just yet. I'd leave that until morning, when I was feeling steadier.

No food, no water skin, no knife, no fire flints. No canvas for shelter. Not one of the items I always packed for our shore expeditions. I had wished for adventure all those years ago as I left England, but not like this.

I curled around Scratch's case, resting my cheek on the damp wood. When I closed my eyes, I felt the motion of the *Beagle* as if I were back aboard, and how I wished I was in my hammock below decks, the creaks of the ship and snores of my crewmates a strange but familiar lullaby. But somehow, there on the black volcanic rock beneath a cactus so spiky I couldn't touch it, I slept.

I emerged from a nightmare of my time overboard – of losing grip of the rope, of my marooning, of the sky beast and my fantastical trip into the air. Something had woken me.

A strange sound – between a growl and a hoot – low and very close. Something touched my leg.

CHAPTER EIGHT

The moon was behind the clouds and all I could make out was a shadow at my feet, a patch of greater darkness big enough to frighten me. Very slowly, I pulled back my foot. Mr Darwin had told me that when faced with a wild animal, it was best to remain still so as not to startle it further. I tried to slow my thumping heart. Well Mr Darwin wasn't here, was he. And he hadn't seen the gigantic sky beast sweep me into the air, so his knowledge wasn't awful helpful right now.

Neither the shadow nor I moved. This was a stand-off – who would strike first? I slowly clutched two handfuls of black dirt then sprung up with a scream, hurling it in the direction of the animal. I was about to run, when the moon left the clouds and I got a better look.

At first, I thought it was one of the marine iguanas. In the moonlight I could see it was a reptile, but smaller than I had thought, more like the size of a large house cat. I blew out a long breath of relief; this creature wasn't going to kill me, at least not easily, though small animals could be surprisingly vicious.

It was using a pair of front claws to rub the dirt from its eyes and its face was tapered, like a fox's. It was definitely some kind of lizard, but it stood high on its legs, which were beneath its body rather than splayed to the sides like the other reptiles of these islands. The moonlight shone off its smooth green scales, more like those of a snake, and a spiked ridge ran the length of its back right to the tip of its long tail. Although I didn't have the education to keep up with all of Mr Darwin's ideas, I'd paid close attention over the last two and a half years as his servant, collecting and observing thousands of animals. I was certain this was not a species of lizard we'd set eyes on before.

I edged back, cradling my fiddle. We stared at each other. Its eyes were large and round, and shone copper in the moonlight.

It took a step towards me, tossed its head and released

that sound again, between a hoot and a growl.

All the creatures we came across either responded to us with blank fear or disinterest. If they knew mankind well, they sensibly fled for their lives. If they had young to defend, they might attack. This lizard did none of those things. It shook its head and released a strange little sneeze. I suddenly wished I hadn't thrown the dirt in its face.

'I didn't mean to hurt you,' I found myself whispering.

The lizard raised its snout and sniffed. Then it stared beyond me, inland, and with a wrenching grind the earth beneath my feet rippled and I staggered to catch my balance, cursing. A spray of glowing orange spurted from the peak of the volcano. The ground quivered again, and an unearthly groan travelled through my bare feet to my chest, then my throat, until it vibrated my jaw and my eyeballs in their sockets.

Stone me, this whole island was a volcano! And it didn't seem to want me here any more than the sky beast did.

When I turned round, the little lizard was stalking away towards the sea. It did not look back.

The ground fell quiet again, but the smoke above the volcano glowed a hellish orange. It was terrible bad luck, to be shipwrecked on an island with a sky beast *and* a volcano.

I laid my head back on Scratch. 'I wonder how fast lava travels,' I said to my waterlogged fiddle.

Was there any chance I would live long enough to find out?

CHAPTER NINE

I woke to the deep blue of dawn and rose up on my elbows as I remembered where I was. Dark smoke and white steam had replaced the spitting orange at the volcano summit, and the ground remained steady. No sign of the sky beast. Could I have imagined it? I wished I had.

The sky lightened enough to make out the horizon, and I scanned it for a sign of the *Beagle*. Nothing, but at least it was calm; good weather for them to search for me. *Things always look better in the morning,* my da always said.

My stomach groaned. On the *Beagle*, breakfast was

served in the mess at eight o'clock sharp. I wondered if the captain would be planning the search for me with Mr Darwin and if the men would talk of me between their spoonfuls of hot oatmeal with dollops of the thick sweet molasses we'd bought in Lima. Robbins would be awful grim about losing me off the rowboat. I swallowed down the thought of them.

There was no sign of anything edible on this scrubland. I stood and rubbed my cheek where the damp wood of Scratch's case had left a clammy cold patch. I still didn't feel ready to open the case and see the ruined instrument, so I strapped Scratch to my back, which gave me some comfort, and tried to think.

The Galapagos shores were rich with fish and turtles, but I had nothing to catch them with. Mr Darwin had eaten iguana, but they were not usually considered edible. I could try to make a spear somehow, but without fresh water the salty sea fish would leave me mighty thirsty.

At least the summit of the volcano showed no sign of activity and the sky was clear of flying beasts. I could wait on the shore but then I'd be in clear view if the beast did come back. I needed a signal, a fire, but for that I'd need wood, and would worry about how to light it later. There wasn't much choice: I set off inland.

The storm had left behind swiftly clearing clouds and

now and again there was a spatter of rain, which I gobbled at greedily. But it wasn't enough, and my mouth was already sticky and sour. What I wouldn't have given for a cup of tea right then. Even better, a cup made by my da. He'd been gone since I was six, but I could still taste the strong tea with the metallic flavour of my own little pewter tankard and the shavings of sugar he saved just for me. My tea days were over when Da died and I went to live with my aunt. She'd have me making tea aplenty, but I'd be lucky if I tasted the cold bottom-pot dregs myself. Nowadays, I was in charge of the tinpot tea which I made over the fire for the master whenever we camped, and there was never a shortage. Through all our expeditions I must have made hundreds of steaming brews.

We'd always had so much kit with us, and now I had nothing. I shook my head at myself. And here I was, thinking about tea.

I reached a lava field and paused. The solid black flow stretched far inland and was smoother than most we'd seen, so at least it wouldn't cut my bare feet completely to shreds. It must have been here for some time because there were pits, and the stout chimneys Mr Darwin called fumaroles. But these ones were long dead, no longer spouting smoke and steam from deep in the earth, and spiky cactuses had sprung up inside and around them. In the distance there might just be a band of greenery I hadn't been able to see yesterday. The sky was still clear, and the volcano calm. As I walked away from the fumaroles, out of the corner of my eye I saw one of the cactus stems wobble. I stopped still, watching. It must have been the wind.

'Well, it's hardly surprising I'm a little nervy,' I said. The sound of my own voice made me feel stronger.

Nervy? You've got the right collywobbles.

The voice in my head was Scratch replying, like the fiddle sometimes did when I berated him for a duff note.

'What if I have, Scratch?' I replied, tugging on the fiddle strap.

Just watch yourself, clumsy clout. I've been through enough.

I smiled and shrugged. Da used to call me a clumsy clout. Then he'd muss my hair and smile, to show he didn't mean it.

As I walked on, I had the sense of something following me. It reminded me of games I played with my neighbours in the lane back home in Bedford; *What's the Time Mr Wolf*?

No, wild animals didn't follow people, not unless they were used to being fed by them, and there were no humans on these islands, as far as we knew. There was a small colony of settlers on Charles Island – Mr Darwin planned to visit the governor there – but I could not imagine a person living in such a godforsaken place as this.

I did have the collywobbles. I was being followed by my own fearful shadow.

CHAPTER TEN

The cactuses that grew on the rough black soil of the inland scrub were different, and my heart soared to see the familiar prickly pears we'd found all over the Galapagos. Remembering the wet sweetness of the fruit made my mouth water, but to harvest one I needed a knife. The cactus itself was coated in a pincushion of needle spikes, and the fruit was thick with spiky hairs that would bring up an itchy rash.

Food, right there, but impossible to get to. There had to be a way.

I scrambled around on the ground and found a stick, little more than a stalk of dry grass. I poked at a fruit and the stick snapped.

That was predictable.

'God loves a trier,' I said through gritted teeth.

I pulled my sleeve down and reached carefully into the gap between the big fleshy leaves, grinning in triumph as I made it without being poked. I pinched my fingers around the stem and twisted. Not a chance. I was not so lucky on the way out. I dragged my hand too fast, and three spines stuck my skin. In the pain, I staggered backwards and fell over.

You clumsy—

'—clout. Yes. I know,' I said, as I pulled the spines from my arm, 'well, at least there's no one here to see . . .'

But I wouldn't mind if the captain's boy, Davis, ribbed me all day for ever more, if only I could see them all again. The *Beagle* was a small cramped ship, with seventy-four men and boys aboard, but Captain Fitzroy was a fair man, and we rubbed along well together. The gruff ship's cook, Phillips, gave me extra raisins with my suet pudding at supper. Laughing Davis, made fun of a duff note on my fiddle but sang a ballad better than anyone. And tough Robbins had four sons of his own back in England and had always looked out for me.

I felt like kicking the prickly pear plant, but didn't want to pincushion my foot as well as my hand. It would be a while before I starved, I reasoned; finding a source of water and somewhere to shelter from the sky beast was more important. To view the island I'd need to find a high point, but climbing a volcano, the highest point around, was not the cleverest of ideas. And climbing without water, when my throat was already dry, would only make my situation worse.

I growled in the back of my throat. I wasn't used to all these decisions. I was used to doing as I was told.

The clouds cleared and the sun began to beat hot. Exhaustion overtook me. I collapsed to the ground and stared at the horizon through the measly shade of another prickly pear cactus, trying to remember how Robinson Crusoe survived. Phillips had brought the book on board and I took turns reading with the handful of other sailors who read well enough to tell a tale aloud. Crusoe had been armed with a musket, knife and cooking pot when *he* was set ashore. Lucky fellow.

I surveyed my fiddle case. It had now dried, and was all I had. If the instrument was completely ruined, I could at least use the case to catch rainwater. I stared up doubtfully at the blue sky. By nightfall, though I could hardly bear to think of this, I might have to use it as fire-wood.

Before I could change my mind, I flipped the catches and split the wax seals of the fiddle case. I hardly dared look. After protecting Scratch so carefully during nearly four years at sea, I was prepared to have my spirits knocked by his wreckage, but instead I broke into a grin that almost cracked my salty sunburnt face. The fiddle was in one piece! I ran my fingers over the felt inside the case. Only slightly damp. I lifted Scratch, smelt his musty comforting old smell, and settled him between my chin and shoulder in his familiar nook. I drew out the bow, tightened the horsehair and took a deep breath.

'Keep me company, Scratch,' I said.

Do you deserve it after all you've put me through?

I grinned and pulled the bow over the strings. It sounded . . . the same. The vibration of the strings started through my jaw and hands, then travelled to settle every muscle in my exhausted body. After a few notes that would have brought tears to Mr Darwin's eyes – and not in a good way – I managed to coax out a lively jig, one I often played to alert the sailors I was about to begin the evening's entertainment.

'Don't fret, Scratch, I'm a bit out of tune myself.'

The fiddle screeched an especially horrid note in reply.

I cautiously wound the pegs.

Mind your manners, young—

I tried the strings again. Almost in tune and not a single broken string. It felt like a miracle. I sat cross-legged and fiddled a jolly sea shanty in celebration, humming along.

For a minute or two I was so lost in the melody I could have been anywhere – at home with Da, busking on the streets of Bedford, in the officers' cabin on the *Beagle*. When I opened my eyes, the green lizard from the previous night stood, head cocked to one side, in front of me.

CHAPTER ELEVEN

I stopped playing my fiddle, mid-bar, and the lizard raised its snout and sniffed. A ruff of spiky scales raised at the back of its neck. I hadn't seen those before, and when they stood on end they looked like a prickly headdress. One scale was missing, leaving a gap. Then the ruff lowered, and it turned away. I quickly played on, and when it flicked its head back round I almost smiled.

The green scales that covered the lizard's body were large, more like those of an armadillo than any reptile I'd seen, and next to the cactuses it was quite camouflaged. Mr Darwin would have called the shade *Pistachio Green*, from the book he liked to use, *Werner's Nomenclature of*

Colours – try getting your tongue round *that* title. But its large eyes were a shade of copper like nothing I'd seen in Werner's book or anywhere else.

As I played on, I thought I saw its fox-like snout dip and rise in time to the music. No, that was impossible.

You're so glad to see something alive, you'd probably fiddle to a flea.

I wasn't going to argue with Scratch on that.

I finished another shanty and laid the violin down in the shade of the cactus to dry out fully. The lizard took a step closer and sniffed. Then it flopped down and laid its snout on its foreclaws.

'So, you liked that, did you?' I asked, not feeling as silly as I should, talking to a lizard. 'Sorry, but I need to let the fiddle properly dry out for now.'

I opened the case to air that too, keeping one eye on the lizard. I'd forgotten about the small compartment at the top, where I kept spare strings and a block of amber rosin for the bow. The strings would be useful – I could find a way to hook a prickly pear or to catch fish – but when I flipped open the lid, something else was in there too, and my heart leapt.

Mr Darwin's eyeglass. I'd snatched it up from the ground as we left the field of giant tortoises just yesterday. What luck! I pressed it to my eye, but it was meant for close work and through it the world in front of me was blurred and wobbly. How I wished Mr Darwin were here. If a gentleman were lost at sea there would be a big to-do to search for him, but a simple cabin boy-turned-servant, with no one at home who'd miss him … perhaps they'd already given me up for lost.

The lizard was still looking at me.

'Yes. You're right, no more of that sort of talk,' I said.

I'd just gained twice as many possessions as I had five minutes ago. This was something to celebrate.

'See this? I've seen men start fire with a magnifying glass.'

You think the Beagle *could spot your smoke against the volcano?*

I turned. The smoke puffing from the top of the volcano was no longer being swept away by the wind and had formed a black pool of cloud above the summit.

'I'll make a fire and then I can cook fish and singe the spikes off the prickly pears,' I retorted. 'I'll have a cheerful blaze going through the night, right on the shore where the lookout will spot me.'

Not going to start anything with these clouds.

It was hot and bright, but had become hazy. No matter! I laid back, hands behind my head, and made myself smile. It was an old trick. Sometimes, when my aunt was in a worse than usual fit and I'd been missing Da something dreadful, I'd smile at strangers in the street and sooner or later someone would smile back, and I'd feel a little better. Just a little.

I lifted my chin. The green lizard was still there. Maybe it was even smiling back, I couldn't tell.

Something always turned up. I'd told myself that when my aunt had locked me in the coal cellar four years ago, and I'd been right. I'd run away and ended up on the *Beagle*.

The sun would soon burn off the haze.

Owww! I squealed in pain and jolted upright. The lizard was right there. I scooted back, clutching my foot. Why – the little brute had bitten me!

CHAPTER TWELVE

I leapt to my feet, hopping away from my attacker and grasping my foot which was stinging awful bad. The lizard must have poison in its bite, maybe venom like a snake. But it wasn't interested in having another go at me, instead it was pawing the ground like a bull about to charge. Something whipped and twisted beneath its claw. A giant centipede. That was the culprit!

The nasty thing was as long as my forearm with a glossy black body and yellow striped legs. It gave a last twitch before it fell still, pinned by the lizard's claw.

The lizard had been defending me.

My whole leg now throbbed, and pain filled my head

like scalding pitch. I collapsed back to the ground and writhed in a fresh surge of agony, as if I were being attacked again. I needed to remember what I knew about this creature. I'd labelled a similar specimen for Mr Darwin a few days earlier; the Galapagos giant centipede. He'd said it could be poisonous. A good reason why, even in the tropical heat, we wore stout boots and gaiters.

The pain came in waves and, when I was able, I angled my foot and forced myself to take a closer look. There were two tiny puncture marks in my heel. A bite. The whole area was already pink and swollen and it felt as if my heart was thumping in my foot.

The lizard nudged the dead centipede, and the scaled ruff at its neck lay flat, its small front teeth showing in a snarl. I shuddered, half expecting the lizard to eat the thing, but it picked it up gingerly with its mouth and flicked the broken insect through the air, and away. Then it ran after it and continued to paw the ground, although the centipede was broken and long dead. The lizard shook its head like a dog shaking off water, and I would have laughed at its outrage if I weren't in such pain. My head thumped and my eyes felt gritty. I tore a strip off the bottom of my ragged trousers and tied it round the bite with numb clumsy fingers. I remembered the ship's surgeon, Mr Bynoe, saying something about sucking out the poison.

I doubled over, forcing my heel to my mouth with a groan, and sucked at the bite then spat on the ground, over and over. I could taste nothing strange, only my own iron blood that now made two fresh red beads on my foot.

Not going to work now. Too late for that.

I curled on the ground, clutching my foot, my body wracked with shakes.

The lizard edged a little closer and lowered itself down beside me, its eyes narrowed. Its irises were like beaten copper, burning bright. But I was feverish, and it was my own eyes that burnt. I closed them and my head spun, as if on a merry-go-round.

I spent the rest of that day and the night racked with shivers, sweats and chills, a pounding tide of pain in my head and foot. I was tormented by nightmares that dragged me back to places I thought I had forgotten – half real, half horrors – conjured up by my poisoned imagination.

My life seemed to play before my eyes. The older sailors said this meant a soul was about to meet its maker, and there was nothing to do about it . . . except make my peace.

'Amazing grace! How sweet the sound . . .' Da sang, and I played the fiddle. The instrument buzzed and tickled

against my small fingers. Then Da's clothes fell empty, collapsed in a dusty pile around me, and the last note all wrong...

'Ungodly child! We took you in for the sake of Christian charity. Jigs and popular music? Only songs of worship will be played under my roof. Little good music did for your father.'

I shrank down on my sleeping mat at Aunt's hearth, holding my fiddle tight. What was Da dying of his winter cough to do with being a fiddler? We'd had cosy lodgings and he'd worked in warm taverns...

Aunt grew and grew until she filled the room, her voice a furious roar. She wrestled my fiddle from my hands and hurled it into the fire. My body was dense as lead, and all I could do was watch the fiddle and my music, Da's music, eaten by flames...

'You have a good ear, young fellow,' said the Naval Recruitment Officer. He flipped a coin into my cap.

'Thank you, sir.'

I played and played, my arms stiff and deep grooves worn into my fingertips. I didn't fancy another night in a shop doorway. I just needed enough coin for a hot pie and a night's board in a decent dosshouse. Passing sailors and their sweethearts tossed in more coins.

The officer was back. 'How old are you, boy?'

'Eleven, sir,' I tried, rolling back my shoulders. I was not yet nine years old but always tall for my age.

'Hmm,' he stroked his ginger whiskers, 'a ship is about to sail, in need of a fiddler. You seem a sturdy sort, if young. Can you work hard, obey orders?'

I nodded. 'That I can, mister. Captain, sir.'

A ship! Fancy me . . . on a ship!

He was gone, and I cringed as hard raindrops bit at my skin. It was not rain, but a stream of coins falling from the sky, filling my cap and rolling across the quayside. I scrabbled to collect them and held one up to see the sun glinting off it. The shiniest new copper farthing . . .

'Farthing,' I croaked, and my own voice woke me.

CHAPTER THIRTEEN

I sat up, wobbly and weak, and my eyes peeled open to see the green lizard in front of me. Staring at me with eyes of new copper. The sun pounding was awful bright.

'Farthing,' I said again.

I uncurled my cramped arms and legs and found the pain in my head had faded. I'd stopped trembling, but my tongue was gummed to the roof of my mouth and I suffered a terrible thirst. There was something pink in the lizard's mouth, and then it was dropped at my feet.

A ripe prickly pear – the spikes removed. It had split, and the juicy contents leaked out. I crawled to the food, my body weak and shaky, scooped out the pink pear flesh with my fingers, and shovelled it into my mouth, seeds and all. The lizard – Farthing – watched.

My stomach grumbled, woken by this morsel. My brain woke up too. This *was* the real world, and I had escaped death. Again. At least for now, because the juice of the fruit reminded me how parched I was.

What a clever little beast this lizard was! To kill the centipede, stay through my illness and now find me food. Only the most intelligent, highly trained dog would do that. Or maybe a counting horse, like the ones at the circus sideshow.

'Do you belong to someone? Are you ... a pet?' I said.

The lizard tilted its head to one side at the sound of my voice.

People living here? Impossible. But wild animals simply didn't behave like this. Except ... I recalled how a pod of porpoises had swam alongside the *Beagle* and Mr Darwin had commented that they seemed to deliberately seek out the company of men.

Was I still half mad with the poison and this whole scene part of my delirium? Well if I was, this was a darn sight better than the nightmares.

'Thank you ... Farthing.'

The lizard tilted its head to the side, and snorted. Then it walked towards the sea, in the direction of the plain of prickly pear cactuses. I checked for the sky beast, then limped after it.

The old sailors were wrong. My life had passed before my eyes, but I was not ready to make peace with my maker – not yet.

After all, I had never been a very peaceful sort of a boy.

CHAPTER FOURTEEN

The sun rose high beneath a white haze, and the air above the earth rippled with midday heat. With no sign of the sky beast I almost convinced myself that I had imagined it, but I still felt its claws wrapped around me, the wind in my face, that drop through the air and the smash into the sea. Farthing stopped at one of the chimney-like fumaroles, as dead as all the others. A fruitless prickly pear sprouted from it and a small black bird pecked at a yellow flower. I noticed this bird's beak was longer and more pointed than those on similar finches we'd observed pecking at mites on the iguanas and tortoises. I was so taken with peering at it, I forgot where I was and almost turned to Mr Darwin to point it out. I'd been with the master so long, it was mighty strange to be alone. Well . . . not completely alone.

I sighed. 'Flowers are good for birds but not for me, Farthing.'

Farthing rested both claws on the rim of the fumarole and gave me a long look.

I shrugged and peered inside. Around the base of the plants was water. The fumarole was a black stone bucket filled with rainwater! I splashed it into my mouth and it was warm and fresh, not salty, and I laughed out loud as I scooped up gulp after gulp until my stomach sloshed.

My reflection stared back at me. My thick black hair was a fright and my dark eyes wild. I'd grown strong in my years at sea, but my ragged clothes and smudged skin made me look like a street waif. Me and the reflection grimaced at each other.

'Well, you really are a useful little thing, aren't you?' I said to Farthing.

The lizard tilted its head to one side and its ruff of spines rose at the back of its neck, like a little coronet. Looking, for all the world, like the animal was proud of itself.

My dull headache began to clear with the water. Even the puncture on my foot felt better as I followed Farthing to the prickly pear field. When it plucked me another fruit, I decided Farthing must be a she. The clue was in her ladylike fruit picking technique. The lizard sniffed at the fruit and chose one of the ripest, pink and yellow, rather than tough green. Smart. Then with a foreclaw all delicate – like the little finger of a fancy lady drinking her tea – the fruit was skewered and twisted from its tough stem. She rolled her prize on the ground to break off the hairs. After, she slit it lengthways with that dainty foreclaw before nudging it with her muzzle towards me. What would Mr Darwin make of her? I thought of the hundreds of specimens we'd preserved in barrels, and shivered.

After gobbling down another three pears, delivered by the little lizard, I felt positively cheerful.

'I am in your debt,' I said with a little bow.

The lizard slowly moved closer. I reached out my hand to her and she watched it approach with narrowed eyes, but she did not move as I touched her on the shoulder, just with two fingers. Her scales felt like overlapping fingernails, nothing like the rough wrinkled skin of the sooty iguanas scattered on the shoreline.

A large dragonfly swept over us and Farthing leapt into the air, clawing at nothing as it darted away, then she fell over on to her back. She seemed to catch sight of her tail and mistake it for the dragonfly because she chased it, snapping and whining, then collapsed to the ground with a snort. I laughed out loud. She looked like . . . a green scaly puppy. She suddenly stopped, shook her head and raised her ruff of scales. She snorted again as if daring me to make fun of her and I pressed my lips together. What a peculiar little creature.

I sighed. For a moment watching Farthing's antics, I'd forgotten my situation. Thanks to the lizard I wasn't going to starve to death just yet, but I still needed to find shelter and the sun still wasn't clear enough to try a fire with the eyeglass.

Rumbles travelled through the ground and then my bones, juddering my teeth, and I turned to see gouts of smoke rising from the summit of the volcano. No spits of red this time, but the ground settled more quickly than my heartbeat did.

I stood and brushed my sticky fingers on my breeches and headed parallel to the shore, just inland from the rocks draped with iguanas. I hoped to find an area of larger rocks or cliffs like we'd seen on other islands, where there might be caves and shelter. Farthing followed me, and I was glad of her company. I wished I could give her something to show she'd done well, that I was grateful for her staying with me and finding food and water, but she didn't need anything from me.

As the afternoon passed, any breeze died along with my hopes of finding a cave. It was back to the tight breathless Galapagos heat, and a band of grey fog squatting over the horizon – the same soupy mist which had made the first visitors call these islands enchanted. Was the fog concealing the *Beagle*? Farthing trotted by my side as I limped back inland through the cactuses, listless now, still weak from the poison. I picked up some dead grass and brushwood to use as kindling later on and stuffed it in the pocket of my breeches. The volcano continued to rumble and release occasional bursts of steam and smoke.

Farthing turned, her ruff flat against her head, and I followed her gaze.

Above the volcano was a black silhouette.

My stomach plummeted as if to make more space for my loud-pumping heart. I told myself it could be a huge hawk, a heron or even an albatross; I'd seen all of these with Mr Darwin on the other Galapagos Islands.

But I knew it wasn't.

CHAPTER FIFTEEN

My scalp and neck prickled, and my legs twitched with the urge to flee. The silhouette of the sky beast hovered above the volcano and then swooped. It was coming for me. Where to hide? I'd never wished to see a tree so much in my life. Farthing sniffed the air, then darted off in a flash of green.

I needed to get down low, but the lizard turned and gave that distinctive hoot, and pawed the ground as if impatient for me to follow.

The black outline of my tormentor was growing bigger. What choice did I have?

Scratch bounced on my back as I ran.

The odd little reptile is our navigator now?

'All right, Scratch! Do you have any better suggestions?' I hissed.

Didn't think so.

The sky beast disappeared over the other side of the volcano. Maybe it hadn't seen me. Farthing picked up her pace and I did the same, my bitten foot throbbing.

We crossed another sloping lava field, heading uphill. This whole island was either lava fields or rough scrubland, could I have landed anywhere worse? We reached a more densely covered area, one of those patches of greenery I'd seen scattering the lower slopes of the volcano. I recognized ferns, and here and there the plants reached my waist. I almost laughed in between my heaving breaths.

'See, Scratch? She's found us some shelter.'

Or is leading us right to the beast.

I crouched low, tugging the fronds of ferns to cover me, and stared up as the sky beast swept high overhead, a silhouette of angular shapes. There was a metallic glint as the sun caught its hide. The day before I'd only been able to make out a giant mass of brutal speed. Now I saw – the sky beast was . . . gold.

Where was Farthing? I mustn't move, even the slightest twitch of the ferns could give me away. The beast passed again, cruising lower, and my heart pummelled so loudly I felt it must give me away. I could think of no living thing with four legs *and* wings, and of that golden sheen. My mind raced. Open eyes, open mind. Birds and bats had wings *instead of* forelegs, Mr Darwin had shown me that. This creature was no real living thing. This creature was from story, from myth.

From myth.

Those spiked wings . . . that almighty size.

No. What with being here alone, the centipede bite . . . I couldn't trust either my eyes or my mind any longer.

I thought of those huge ancient bones, the fossils that fascinated Mr Darwin. That was what the master called hard evidence. Those enormous animals were *real,* or at least they had been once.

Creatures of myth were not.

My heart thumped and then Farthing's green fox-snout nosed through the ferns.

'Shhh! Keep still, or you'll give me away,' I whispered.

I wasn't completely concealed here, but I didn't dare stand to see if there was thicker shelter ahead. It would be a risk to go any further.

Farthing pawed the ground with one claw and growled.

No! I shook my head, pinching my lips together.

She disappeared again, between the ferns, then came back and scuffed at the ground once more, this time flattening the ruff at the back of her head. I remembered that gesture from her attack on the centipede.

Danger. She wanted me to follow her.

I peered upwards. I couldn't see the sky beast between the fronds. But maybe Farthing knew I wasn't concealed enough, wasn't safe . . .

It is a lizard.

Yes. A lizard who knows this island. I crawled on hands and knees behind Farthing, as she threaded on through the low ferns again, ploughing a narrow path for me.

The ferns were thinner here, I should have stayed where I was. I could clearly see the volcano ahead, and the creature was hovering above it, like a hawk watching its prey, black against the glowing orange smoke cloud.

Should I have trusted Farthing to help me in the face of this giant beast?

CHAPTER SIXTEEN

If I had laid flat and stayed completely still, covered by the ferns, I might just have had a chance. Yet here I was, stumbling over the bare lava field once more, chasing a green lizard much faster than I was, in clear view of the sky beast . . . and it had seen me. It swooped in lazy circles above.

Farthing sped along so fast her claws were a blur. She had spotted the flying beast too but she was so small, she'd be less than a mouthful for it. So, what was she doing?

'By the stones, Farthing, where are you leading me?' I whispered, panting.

Farthing was just an animal, she didn't have reason, and I'd been a fool to follow her. But my stride widened to keep up.

Too late.

The beast dived towards us.

I had no idea what the lizard was doing now because she was running *towards* the beast, not away. I was following at full pelt, even though I knew I'd taken leave of my senses! My lungs were bursting, my foot throbbing.

I glanced up and my breath caught.

It was the best view I'd had of the beast yet and it *was* what I had thought it was, what I had known it was . . . but it wasn't possible. I had eaten and slept and it was daylight, so it couldn't be a nightmare, could it?

Which meant it *was* a myth. A myth come to life.

I was being stalked by a dragon.

Yes, a *dragon*.

Now it seemed it had been blindingly obvious all along.

Its scales glistened in the sunlight, gold as a sovereign. Its four legs were powerful, and its wings were bigger than the main rig on the *Beagle*, yet thin enough that the sunlight shone through from above, deep bronze.

I gaped as it streamed past, my legs pumping as if they'd forgotten how to stop, the wind in its wake chasing water from my eyes. Soon it would either kill me or snatch me up to drop me into the sea again, or on the rocks, or just crunch me to bone broth in its claws. Even if – for whatever strange reason – it toyed with me like last time, I'd now been weakened by the centipede poison and surely wouldn't survive another ducking.

I'd be killed by the only dragon in the world – if there were others, even folks like me would have heard of them – and no one would even know what happened. I supposed, as deaths went, at least it was interesting.

But I was determined to live.

My legs found new life as I wove at top speed after Farthing, ducking as the air from the beast's wings buffeted me. We hit another patch of vegetation, but only grass and low ferns, nowhere to hide. Any second I'd be swept into the air.

Well I wasn't going to make it easy for the beast, not this time. It came for me head on, its wings tucked back, like an almighty golden spear. The speed of it! I needed to keep my nerve. Use what I had.

I was small, and small things are difficult to get hold of.

The dragon's claws extended, its wings opened, and I knew what I had to do. When it lunged, I ducked and rolled to the side, then sprang to my feet and kept running. The monstrous claws gouged the ground just to my right, ripping out ferns. With a bellowing shriek it swooped off behind me, the sound ringing in my ears.

It wouldn't take long for it to gain height, turn, and come at me from behind, and I didn't know if I could dodge it again. But my triumph gave me strength. I picked up pace, still following the path Farthing had made for me through the vegetation. She stopped and turned. I risked a glance behind and, just as I suspected, the dragon was back up in the sky and making an arrow-straight line for me. I could already feel those claws, and every hair on my body stood on end with dread.

Last time it had dropped me in the sea. Three times! Why? Because it didn't want me on this island, it had to be. And yet here I was. I hadn't got the message, hadn't heeded the warning. This time it would kill me for sure.

Farthing stopped so quickly, I almost tripped as I raced on past her – and then the ground beneath my feet was . . . gone.

I screamed as the earth swallowed me.

CHAPTER SEVENTEEN

My legs circled in the air and my arms grasped at
nothing. I was engulfed in darkness, then hit
the ground with a thump.

I lay on my back, winded and gasping for breath, and
stared up at the hole I'd fallen through. It was around ten
foot up and lined with grass. The opening wasn't big
enough for the dragon to get to me, but it might force a
claw down here, like a blackbird's beak pecking into the
ground for a worm. I scuttled out of the pool of light and
into the shadows.

Now I saw what that little green lizard had been up to.
Farthing must have known about this hole and led me

here to be safe from the beast, the dragon. But where was she now?

An unearthly scream ripped through the air, a shriek like a banshee or some other horror from a penny dreadful pamphlet, and then flames billowed through the opening above. I sprang to my feet and stumbled back into the darkness finding I was in a tunnel, then turned to watch from a safe distance.

This inferno could not be caused by the volcano. This was pure, burning fire ballooning in great clouds of yellow and orange. My eyes stung and my skin tingled in the heat.

Dragon.

Fire. Breathing. Dragon.

Another screech and the flames continued to swirl and rush, a hissing hungry cascade, pummelling the floor of the tunnel until it glowed red.

'Farthing!' my voice was lost over the roar of the blaze.

She'd brought me to safety and then . . . I spun, searching the tunnel for a sign of her, but I'd have seen—

Farthing wasn't here. She was out there, I'd almost tripped over her when I fell.

Little lizard like that. Be burnt to cinders.

With a final scalding lick at the cave floor, the flames disappeared.

A gust of scorching air hit my face, and I pictured the beat of wings.

Silence. I collapsed back against the cave wall. Farthing. I had to accept she had been directly in the path of the flames. It wasn't fair, she'd brought me here, and she'd saved me. My eyes blurred, I pulled in ragged breaths and then coughed them back out again in the smoke. What were those dots of shattered light? I rubbed my eyes with my fists. The red-hot rock of the cave floor was cooling to black, circled by patches of moss, alight. Fire. I could hardly think for the shock, but I knew I needed fire.

I scrambled at my pocket with shaking hands to fetch out the kindling I had picked up earlier and fed the small fire furthest away from the hole above. There were scraps of scrub around that must have fallen from above, and I crawled around to fetch them all up, moving like a clockwork automaton I'd once seen in a shop window, my mind on Farthing.

When I had used everything that could be burnt, save the clothes on my back, I sat by the flame and clasped my hands together to stop them shaking. A dragon. A dragon.

I swallowed. I could still see the inferno behind my eyelids, that last dart of Farthing's glossy green scales.

I forced myself to look around me.

I was in a tunnel, one of the lava tubes Mr Darwin had warned me about. It stretched two ways, towards the sea and towards the volcano. I remembered what my master had said: 'the lava tubes often run only inches beneath the surface above in places. So, we must be very cautious of falling into one.'

But my fall had been no accident. It had saved me.

Farthing had ... I swallowed.

It was just a lizard. A plain ordinary creature . . .

'No! Stop it! Stop . . .' my voice echoed in the cave and I covered my ears, although I knew Scratch was in my head, as well as on my back.

I slapped my hand against the wall of the tunnel, hard enough to smart, and the pain helped to keep the tears behind my eyes from falling. Getting attached to a lizard, talking to a fiddle . . . I needed to come to my senses. But how could I? I was going to die here, either trapped inside the earth or burnt to ash outside.

I rubbed my face hard. It wasn't over yet. I was thirteen years old and had been at sea for four years. I might not be a man, but I had some wits about me.

That's more like it.

I clenched my teeth.

The hole was too high for me to climb back up and anyhow, I was certainly safer down here for now. I sat by the fire, warming my hands through force of habit, but after nearly being burnt to a crisp it wasn't surprising it didn't give me any comfort.

The tiny blaze soon burnt down and there was nothing more to add to it. I felt the fiddle case strap across my chest. Scratch, made of wood, all dried out.

Don't you dare . . .

I shook my head. 'Then I really would be alone,' I said. My words echoed.

I stared up at the burnt black edges of the hole, and for a second a small green face blinked down at me. But it disappeared with a blink, because it had never been there at all.

Don't even think about it. Nothing could survive a flame like that.

'I wasn't,' I snapped, trying not to think at all, 'but you don't know for sure do you, you . . . didn't see . . .'

My throat swelled. I waited in the heavy silence, then took the fiddle off my back. I opened the case, took out the instrument and played the two songs Farthing had seemed to listen to, her head on one side, her ruff of scales rising.

The floor trembled below me and the earth released a deep groan. Dust settled on me from the roof of the tunnel. I smelt sulphur and wondered if this was going to be my grave, but I played on.

I didn't notice my tears start, just that my face was wet

when I finished. I smudged my hand over my eyes and cheeks and drew a ragged breath. Even Scratch had nothing to say.

CHAPTER EIGHTEEN

Some time later I stood, brushed myself off and put Scratch back in his case. I wound Mr Darwin's eyeglass on its elastic around my wrist and gave one last glimpse up at the blue sky through the hole above, before I turned towards the darkness of the tunnel.

I had no clue which way I should go. Both directions were yawning black mouths. Farthing would have known. I stared into the darkness. The lizard was only with me for a day and a half, I needed to stop feeling so wretched about her being gone.

Quite right. After all, you've collected hundreds of animals just like that one. Many are now preserved in barrels . . .

'None like Farthing,' I snapped.

There was no way to climb out and the tunnel leading to the sea might fill with water if it went any deeper or if there were another storm. The other way, towards the volcano, might fill with lava.

I pressed my forehead with the heel of my hand. I didn't even know for sure which way was which, not after my fall.

Then both are as good as each other.

'Might be the best way of looking at it,' I said.

When the light of the hole faded behind me, the path ahead was black as tar. I should have thought to make a torch of some kind when I'd had the fire, instead of just sitting there like a fool watching it burn. I fumbled along the uneven curve of the tunnel wall, stubbing my toes and grazing my feet on the rough floor. This was useless. But as I was preparing to turn back, there was a slice of light up ahead. I sped up in the gloom, which was about a hundred times better than pitch black, imagining the source of the light to be an exit back to the surface. I might be safe down here from the beast . . . I still couldn't quite believe it – the *dragon* – but I was too well hidden. I would never be found by the crew . . . never. I peered up, and when light fell across my face I felt a burst of energy. The rays of sunlight came from a narrow crack in the ceiling. But it was way too high for me to reach, even

if the gap had been big enough to wriggle through –
which it was not.

I continued on, but soon the darkness was too much
for me. No further cracks in the tunnel roof meant I
could see nothing, no difference when my eyes were
open or closed. Sakes alive! If the captain and Mr
Darwin thought the land here was hellish, these tunnels
had to be purgatory. A place of darkness and waiting and
not knowing what would happen next, and that awful
not knowing lasting for ever and ever.

I couldn't believe I'd ever been excited at the idea of
these lava tubes, or desperate to explore them. Even the
sound of my own breath seemed ragged and frightening.
Shapes formed deep in the dark, shadows followed me
although I knew there was nothing there. Time to turn
back before I lost my mind. I stumbled on a rock, and
stopped. A rock? I felt around on my hands and knees.
There were a few, scattered around the floor of the
tunnel. I picked it up. If I could find enough of them and
build them into a pile, I could climb out of the same hole
I'd fallen in. I smiled for the first time, and the surge of
excitement and relief at having a plan pounded in my ears.

I stood. That sound wasn't my breath or my pounding
heart. It was whispering, hissing, swishing, and getting
closer . . . now there were high squeaks, like a herd of
panicked mice.

My heart seemed to batter its way up to my throat. I'd thought myself already scared, but when something soft brushed against my ear I lost any sense I had left, and screamed.

CHAPTER NINETEEN

I charged headlong down the tunnel, taking huge strides, crashing into the walls, my only thought to get away – *away* – from the squeaking, flapping, fluttering mass that surrounded me, that filled my mouth and nose with a choking sour stench, and set my eyes streaming.

Bats. Only bats.

I knew Scratch was right; we'd seen bat caves in South America, vast clouds bursting out from the mountains at sunset. Of course there would be bats in the lava tubes, it was the perfect home for them. But reason couldn't stop me running, couldn't stop my body believing it was being chased by an army of murderous squealing demons of the dark. There were so many of them, all around me. Some part of me said I should stop and just let the colony fly on past, but the rest of me was determined to run for my life. So I kept on, arms wrapped over my head covering my ears against their piping squeals, their bodies and sharp wings brushing against my legs, arms, face, until it seemed I must have run too far, missed the light of the crack in the ceiling and the hole I had fallen through. But still I raced on, until the cloud of tiny bodies thinned out and I staggered to a stop and collapsed to the floor, arms still shielding my head. The last stragglers fluttered past and I flinched until there was finally silence and the pounding in my ears began to fade. Except it didn't, quite. There was still pounding, but it was from outside. The sea?

I unfolded myself and found I was no longer in total darkness. The black had become grey.

I shook my head as one solitary bat squeak remained, piping like the nest of sparrows in the chimney at my aunt's place, before she got at them with a broom.

I scanned around the tunnel, goosebumps rising. Maybe the sound was lodged in my ears now, because I couldn't see the source of it . . .

Movement by my feet made me start back, still jumpy. A flutter. I crouched and saw it was a lone bat, and very tiny, with a body half the size of a house mouse, covered in red-brown fur, with a flattened little face.

'Minutes ago, I'd been terrified . . . of you. But you're just a helpless little scrap,' I whispered.

Well, I couldn't just leave it there. I scooped it up and it squeaked more loudly and wriggled, then fell silent. Had I scared it to death? I shifted it to the palm of one hand. Its black wings were rumpled and I gently spread them – there didn't seem to be any injury. It might be a new species that only lived in these tunnels, one of the animals that made Mr Darwin so interested in the Gala-pagos.

Without warning, the bat sprung from my hands, fluttered haphazardly around my head, then flew into the tunnel beyond, disappearing where the passage began to widen.

I stared after it, then began to walk. After a few paces I stopped. Ahead of me the tunnel opened into a cave – and beyond that must be where the light was coming from. A way out! But my eye was drawn to something else.

Shapes, in the gloom. A dull glint. The cave was not empty.

PART THREE

*. . . the different islands to a considerable extent
are inhabited by a different set of beings.*

CHARLES DARWIN, *JOURNAL OF RESEARCHES*

CHAPTER TWENTY

I scanned around the cave in the gloom. A coil of rope. A pile of wood. A jumble of rags and leather. A chest. The glint I'd first spotted was from old metal.

Humans had been here, in this cave.

The metallic gleam came from a knife. I picked it up, unable to believe my eyes or my luck. It was ancient, mostly tarnished to black, but with this I would be able to eat as many prickly pears as I wanted. I stopped still, remembering how Farthing had plucked them with her claw, then shook my head, trying not to think about it. Other items had mouldered away and I couldn't make out what they had once been. My eyes lingered on a heavy timber chest, coated in pitch with tarnished brass clasps.

Could I really have come across a buccaneer's treasure hoard? After all, no dragon story was complete without gold. I found a sturdy rock and tapped against the catches to loosen them, visions of the glowing coins filling my head.

And what exactly are you going to do with gold?

'What does anyone do with gold?' I said. My voice didn't echo here, as if the ancient items were sucking in the sound.

I wiped my brow on my ragged neckerchief, and prised the knife into the edge of one of the clasps. Flakes of rust fell away. I worked at the other fastening and threw it open. The lid of the chest slammed back on its hinges – it was as empty as my stomach and my hope of rescue. I sighed, then ran my hand around the smooth dry interior of the box.

The floor shook again, and this time the tremors continued on, and on. I crouched and covered my head with my hands as dust rained down on me. I didn't know enough about volcanoes; I hadn't listened hard enough when Mr Darwin and the other gents had discussed the geology of these islands.

The earth gave a last shaky belch, then the rumbling stopped. The ceiling seemed intact at least, although how much longer it would hold in these earthquakes I didn't want to think about.

I needed to be above ground.

Behind the chest something caught my eye.

What now? Stay here any longer and we'll be sharing a grave.

'I just need to look . . .' I muttered.

It was a mound, covered in rags, dust rising from it. I stepped over the mouldering ropes and shifted aside canvas, stiff and blackened in places, to reveal wooden planks. No, not planks, curved wooden slats. It took a long moment to make sense of what I was seeing.

It was a better find than any treasure.

A boat.

A tiny boat, face down, resting against the wall of the cave. I pushed the canvas completely to the floor. There were no obvious holes in the wood, although it was crumbling in places. Some of the pitch that must once have coated it was worn away, but it looked remarkably sound, considering.

A boat. On this island there was a fire-breathing dragon, an active volcano and no fresh water supply. Sending a fire or smoke signal wasn't going to be enough, or even possible, what with the dragon having me in its sights.

What I really needed was to escape. And now I could.

What was I waiting for? The light meant there must be a way out and now I had a *boat*. I grinned. I lifted the chest – how I'd ever thought it could contain gold I did not know, it was far too light – then slung the coil of rope over my shoulder, releasing clouds of spinning dust motes. I turned the boat over and felt my grin widen. It did seem to be whole. A little scrap of a thing, more like the rowboat a child would use to go fishing than the solid craft we used for our shore excursions from the *Beagle*. How had a boat so small ended up here—

My eyes tracked back into the space against the wall where it had been. My heart froze and I backed away, hand over my mouth.

A seated figure wearing a tricorn hat.

CHAPTER TWENTY-ONE

The head of the buccaneer was tipped forward, his tricorn hat thick with dust, his body wrapped in more of the stained canvas, like a shawl. I let out an awkward squeak of shock, as I imagined an undead swashbuckler leaping up to ambush me, cutlass waving, before my good sense won the battle and my heart slowed.

I edged forward slowly, passing around the boat to get a closer look. I did not touch, simply bent to peer beneath the rim of the hat and then ducked back gasping after catching a glimpse of his jaw.

Whether it were skin or bone, it looked like tanned

leather. He'd been dead a very long time. Maybe he had been sealed in here and the earthquakes had only recently created a way out. That would be why the animals hadn't got to him, and he'd mouldered away. Shivers ran up and done my spine and I made a sign of the cross.

There was plenty of real danger here – from the fire-breathing dragon and any other poisonous biter, to the groaning earth and spitting volcano.

This fellow is the least of your worries.

'Well forgive a boy for being a bit shaken, finding a corpse in a dark cave and all,' I said.

I crouched down in front of the buccaneer and whispered, 'I don't suppose you are going to be needing this boat any time soon, sir?'

The dead buccaneer said nothing. Thankfully.

The boat might need a few repairs, and I wouldn't know if it was watertight until I tried it in the sea. As I scrambled around the cave floor for anything else that might be useful, I wondered what had happened to the dead man. Had he been set adrift from a ship of buccaneers as a mutineer, left to fend for himself on an island with no source of water? Why would a sailor be marooned with an empty chest – one so sturdy, expensive in its day. Maybe he had become ill – the smallpox? – and been left by his crewmates so as not to contaminate the whole ship. I didn't fancy investigating him further, he had curled up in peace beneath his boat, hat over his eyes, to die, and it wasn't my place to disturb him now.

I found a green-black copper pan among the buccaneer's belongings. Aside from the knife and the coil of rope, there didn't seem to be anything else of use, and I stowed them in the base of the boat along with a tiny oar.

This man had died down here alone. I was suddenly very keen to get out of these hellish tunnels, dragon or not. But I lingered, wondering how long he'd survived here before—

What are you waiting for? Nothing you can do for him.

'There is one thing,' I said.

Once more I lifted my fiddle from its case and played the hymn I had played at Da's funeral. I wondered how old this man had been. My da hadn't yet been thirty when the consumption took him. I sang the words in my mind as I drew the bow across the strings, gripping Scratch tight to my chin.

Amazing grace! How sweet the sound,
That saved a wretch like me!
I once was lost, but now am found,
Was blind, but now I see.

The words rang in my head as the last note faded.

'Not found *yet*,' I said firmly, and packed Scratch away.

I slid the boat back into the darkness and rushed along the rest of the tunnel towards the light.

The passageway grew narrow, sloping uphill, the sound of the sea was louder and amber sunlight soaked into me, filling me with energy. It must be nearing sunset. I stood before the cave exit, a wide crack leading to the outside. I remembered how the dragon fire had billowed into the hole.

I couldn't take any chances. I had a boat now, but I needed to live long enough to use it.

I ducked out, peered upwards first, scanning the sky for signs of the dragon. The sun was setting, and high strips of clouds caught the rosy rays like cheerful pennants. I gazed around me, only daring to dip the top of my head out of the hole. In front, I couldn't see an awful lot, as black boulders blocked my view. I heard the sweep of the sea from that direction. Behind me, the volcano was spurting lazy gouts of liquid and I imagined lava bubbling in a great pool at its summit, like jam left too long on the stove. Da was good with jam, I remembered – he used my ma's own recipe. My ma had fallen ill in the autumn just after I was born, and making the jam always made Da twist his wedding ring even more than usual. I sighed. Not the perfect time for memories.

Despite the spitting volcano, the earth was quiet . . . but probably not for long.

I scrambled across the rocks to find a dark gravel beach laid out with glossy brown and grey mounds, many laying still, others lumbering slowly or rolling, sometimes over the top of one another. We'd seen these animals on every island we'd been to – sea lions. One noticed me and looked up. It had beady black eyes and a dog-like muzzle with a spiky moustache of white whiskers.

'Huh. Will you look at that?' I said beneath my breath.

An almighty bellow made me almost leap out of my skin.

CHAPTER TWENTY-TWO

I spun around to come face to face with a sea lion, much bigger than any of the others, rising high on his front flippers, a mound of gleaming muscular bulk. He had a lump in the middle of his forehead and his whiskered snout was drawn back in a snarl, baring a fearful set of sharp orange teeth. An ugly cut striped across his muzzle and clouded one eye.

Mr Darwin's voice came back to me: 'The bull sea lions guard their territory closely, Covington, they'll fight for hours, and their wounds can be fatal. It isn't unknown for them to mistake a man for an unwelcome interloper out to steal his females, so take good care.'

I raised both hands and edged backwards, almost tripping over one of the bodies – probably the female this furious male sea lion mistakenly thought I was after.

'Whoa there! I don't mean any trouble, big fellow. Just let me get out of your way . . .'

Another bellow, this time from behind, and I turned to see a second male rearing up. He too had gashes across his muzzle and a clear set of claw marks across his chest.

I'd stumbled directly into the middle of a sea lion brawl.

The two bull sea lions crashed down on to the sand. I didn't know if they were furious at me, or only at each other, or both. I crouched, trying to make myself look less of a threat. But the movement disturbed the sea lion to my left, and he took a swipe at me with his huge flipper, slapping me across the shoulder and sending me sprawling on to my back. He thumped down on his belly, unbalanced by the swipe, and I only just rolled out of the way as his quivering bulk sent vibrations through the sand.

I scooted backwards, out of the space between the two sea lions, and crawled on hands and knees away, but now the one who had swiped my shoulder had his attention firmly on me. He was quicker than he looked, galloping towards me on those front flippers. I scrambled to my feet but slipped, and he gained on me, grunting . . . and then a different sound threaded through the hollers, something between a hoot and growl.

A flash of green sprang from nowhere on to the sea lion's head. A pair of claws covered his eyes and his ear was gripped between a set of small pointed teeth.

Farthing!

CHAPTER TWENTY-THREE

It really *was* Farthing! She tugged the sea lion's ear like a puppy playing with a knot-end of rope, and the animal waddled in a frantic circle, flicking his head from side to side and bellowing. I scrambled to my feet and back up the rocks I'd climbed to reach this beach. The smaller sea lion took his opportunity; whilst his opponent was distracted he lunged, slamming into the larger animal's body and rolling right over his tail; they were like the mud wrestlers I'd once seen at the harvest fair.

'Farthing!' I called out, terrified she would be crushed.

Farthing sprang free and darted towards me and was almost safely away when the bigger animal whipped around and launched himself after her. I gasped as the sea lion bit down on the end of the lizard's tail.

'Farthing! Run, now! Here . . . Farthing!'

Farthing was flung to the ground but bounced back up, twisting to bite the fleshy lump between the sea lion's eyes. He shook his head with more booming bellows and Farthing was flicked free. She landed neatly and raced up to where I stood on the rocks, continuing past me and over the pile.

I ran after her. The very end of her spiky tail had been bitten clean off leaving a bloody stump. I stopped at the crack where I'd emerged from the cave and pointed. Farthing was injured and should take shelter, but she didn't stop running.

This time I didn't question that the lizard knew where she was going, I simply couldn't bear to let her out of my sight. It dawned on me that she was still the only one of her kind I had seen. Maybe this lizard wasn't Farthing at all.

I stopped. The lizard stopped and nudged at the ragged stump of her tail with her snout. I crouched as she turned. Those bright copper eyes. She tilted her head to one side and the ruff of scales at her neck rose. One of the scales was missing from the neat row.

'It really is you,' I whispered. Somehow, she'd survived the fire. My throat felt full and I had an urge to sweep her up in my arms, but instead I reached out my open hand. Farthing took a step forward and nudged her snout gently into my palm.

'That was awful bricky, taking on those big beasts,' I said, and stroked her scales.

I looked up at the purple-pink evening sky. Still no sign of the dragon, but I needed to get Farthing underground with me. But the relief at seeing her again made me feel weak and dizzy. I was tired of trying to figure out the best thing to do, so I followed her.

Farthing led me inland through a plain of prickly pears, and I stopped, my mouth watering. I'd left the buccaneer's knife in the boat.

She stopped and pawed at the ground, impatient, turning only her head to look behind.

'I need to eat,' I said, picking up a stone and tapping it against a ripe fruit, avoiding the irritating hairs. Farthing huffed out a noisy breath, but with the help of her tough claws, I ate until I was full. My shoulder was throbbing. I peered behind me and saw my shirt was ripped. There was a gash where the sea lion had struck me, and it was oozing blood that had soaked into my already filthy shirt. Farthing raised her snout and sniffed. Then she ran on.

I blew out a long breath. I couldn't follow her for ever; the red sun was nearly touching the horizon. I needed to get back to the tunnel and shelter until sunrise.

I imagined Mr Darwin in his cramped cabin on the *Beagle*, table strewn with papers, eyes shadowed with worry. Captain Fitzroy wouldn't want a further delay to the voyage; he didn't think much of the Galapagos and had said he was keen to leave. Tomorrow, I would test the tiny boat.

Any thoughts about navigating? The lizard can't help you there.

I didn't reply to that, but realized I was blindly following the little lizard yet again.

'Where are you going, Farthing?' I said. She was now heading alongside the shoreline. The ground was flattened and dotted with pale pinkish blotches – hundreds, maybe thousands of them – reaching way into the distance. What were they?

Farthing stopped at the edge of this flatter area and I slipped, smacking down on the seat of my pants into something thick, cool and slimy.

CHAPTER TWENTY-FOUR

I sat up straight, afraid of sinking sand or a swamp, and released a squeak of shock. A huge pink bird looked down its crooked black beak at me, like a rose-coloured swan whose legs had grown too long. It wasn't scared of me, and stopped to take a delicate sip of water from a pool in the mud before stalking off on its spindly legs, like a lady holding her skirts out of the town filth. And now I saw that the blotches were a giant flock of these birds. I wondered if they were edible. My stomach would love some meat, those prickly pears didn't satisfy for long. The bird cocked its head like it had read my mind.

'No fear, Mr Pink. The knife is back at the tunnel, and I think you'd be safe even if I had it,' I said. We were on a kind of floodplain or salt marsh, stretching out to the sea at a distance. Sally Lightfoot crabs skittered across the surface of the black mud. It reminded me of when Da took me to the Thames Flats to see if the sea air might help his cough. We'd collected cockles on a hot afternoon, cooked them in a pot over a driftwood fire, and eaten them hot and fresh, spicy with vinegar.

I sighed at the memory. Imagine what Da would have made of this place. He'd toured with a band, before I came along, and always said when I was old enough we'd travel together.

The pole-legged birds were scattered across this mud field in their thousands. I scanned the sky, but found no sign of the dragon. For now. The ground trembled and I fixed my eyes on the volcano. The smoke was thick above it and a spray of orange lava spurted into the air. A scattering of birds flew off in a giant cloud of white and pink, and then landed again further along the shore. The ground steadied, but the volcano definitely looked angrier.

'What are you up to?' I said, when I saw Farthing wallowing in the sludge like a pig. She burrowed her snout in a muddy pool and blew thick bubbles. I laughed.

'Have you brought me here to play?' I said, and as I said it, I remembered the local people we'd stayed with at Tierra de Fuego in South America. They'd made a poultice of straw and mud . . .

Could Farthing have brought me here for healing? I leant down, dipped my finger in the black mud, and sniffed it. It wasn't rotten, didn't smell of much at all, just earth and sea. I reached over and smeared some across the wound on my shoulder while Farthing watched me. It didn't feel good or bad, maybe a bit cooler. I shrugged. When I'd finished, she sniffed the air in my direction. She was satisfied.

What a clever and strange little beast she was.

Darkness was falling now. I turned and started back towards the opening that led into the tunnel. I checked Farthing was behind me, she followed at a distance. I reached the gap and ducked through into the tunnel. I waited for my lizard friend and wondered what I would do if she didn't follow. I couldn't force her to stay with me and I had nothing to tempt her.

After all your maudlin, the creature wasn't even dead.

Scratch was propped up by the boat.

I stared up at the entrance to see Farthing's bright copper eyes peering down at me.

The memory of the dragon filling the hole with flame billowed into my mind and I wanted to run up there, grab her close and keep her with me. But I just watched. She glanced this way and that, then gave a small hoot and slipped through the gap to join me.

This time it was Farthing who had followed me.

CHAPTER TWENTY-FIVE

I slept near the opening of the tunnel, far from the long-dead buccaneer. Farthing stayed close, her head rested on her claws, her tail – its bitten end now crusted in dried mud – curled around her. Her eyes didn't close, but they narrowed to slits.

The blue light of sunrise woke me. This must be my fourth morning on the island.

The Beagle *could be long gone by now.*

I swallowed and forced myself not to think about it.

'Well, who's being maudlin now?' I said. 'I've got a boat to launch.'

Farthing's eyes flicked open wide at the sound of

my voice.

That night it had rained, and I'd left the buccaneer's tarnished copper pan out for this very reason. As I drank away my thirst, the ground trembled, but it had become a bit like my aunt's complaints; happening so often I hardly noticed it.

I hauled the boat up and out with the rope I'd found. I knew better than to stumble into sea lion territory again and dragged it sideways along the smooth rock until I reached the flamingo mud flats beyond. It was difficult to keep to my feet here and I slipped over more than once in the black mud, Farthing hooting each time and nudging me. Having the small lizard there kept my spirits up, even though, in the light of day, the ancient boat seemed a mean thing and I was fearful it wouldn't float at all.

Eventually I reached the shoreline, shoulders burning with effort.

The water was shallow and without rocks. I waded out and the boat lifted. Afloat. I sat inside it and a few tiny spouts of water jumped from the seams, with one little fountain wide enough to give me serious worry. Any sailor would eye it with disgust, especially without a ship's swain to do a day's work on it. I imagined how Robbins would grimace at the sight of it, he'd probably give me a gentle cuff around the ear for even suggesting it was seaworthy. Its seams needed filling or it wouldn't float for long. If I was forced to bail out constantly, I'd not be able to row and would be going nowhere.

I climbed out and looked at Farthing, as I tugged on my neckerchief trying to think of a solution. In the high sun, the lizard's eyes glowed metal-bright. I scratched my back where the mud had cracked and the wounds were crusting over underneath. It didn't feel too bad.

The animals on this island used what they had. What did I have? The buccaneer's boat, rope, knife and pan. Mr Darwin's eyeglass, the clothes on my back . . .

Forgetting something?

Of course! Scratch, and my block of rosin in the case. Rosin was pine resin, waxy and waterproof.

I hauled the boat up the mud and on to the dry lava field. The timber would dry quickly in the midday heat and then I'd fix it as best I could. The ground shifted with a deep groan. Farthing lifted on her hind legs. I'd not seen her do that before and I laughed, until I saw she was sniffing in the direction of the volcano.

She was right, there was an awful bad smell, like when the ship's cook had burnt an ostrich egg that was going to be the captain's breakfast. The volcano was spitting and smoking.

Then Farthing released a call that was more growl than hoot, and raced off in the direction of the volcano so fast her legs were a blur. I searched the sky for the dragon, remembering the last time she'd run off like this she'd been leading me to safety in the lava tube. But there was no dark shape in the sky.

I watched her run like a small green dart, skimming over the rocks until she was in amongst the prickly pears and I could no longer make her out. I felt hollow. She was a lizard, a wild animal, I would never know what she was thinking and I couldn't expect her to remain at my side all the day.

Farthing came back before, she'd come back again.

Not like you can take her with you, anyway.

I didn't have anything to say to that.

I smoothed the rosin into the seams between the boat slats as the sun beat mercilessly on my head and neck, then left my handiwork to set in the shade of a rock and brought the copper pot, the knife and Scratch up from the cave. I couldn't just leave with no provisions at all. I needed water, food.

I stared out to sea. It was flat now and there was no wind. If only I could make it back to Albemarle. If the *Beagle* had already left I had a chance of survival there, on the largest island, with a supply of fresh water. The currents were difficult in the channels between islands and I would likely be swept into open ocean. I was no navigator, but Robbins had taught me to find my way using the stars. How would that help me when I had no way to steer, though?

Stay bricky.

One thing at a time.

At least with the knife I could collect prickly pears myself. I stared along the wide horizon and back at the tiny boat.

Mr Darwin's eyeglass was still wound around my wrist and the sun was burning. I didn't need to leave right away. I should set a fire on the beach, it was a clear day and if the *Beagle* did pass by . . .

You're waiting for the lizard.

I didn't have an answer to that either.

CHAPTER TWENTY-SIX

I filled my mind with the task of creating fire, collecting driftwood from the mud pools, and leaving the twigs and scraps to dry on the rock. I sharpened the knife to a keen silver edge with a stone, then used it to shave threads off the end of the rope until I had a little pile. Over these I added a steeple of sticks.

Not going to manage much fire with that.

'I'm only trying it now, and if it works I can forage inland for more wood later.'

Sounds like a good excuse to search for the lizard.

It was true, I couldn't stop thinking about Farthing and how she'd darted off so suddenly. Where had she gone? I took Mr Darwin's eyeglass and squeezed it tight in my hand. The young gentleman said he saw nature's magic through that glass.

I tilted the lens back and forth in the sun, finally concentrating a thin beam, until my pile of kindling began to smoulder. I laughed out loud. I hadn't expected it to actually work! I held the beam steady as I crouched over it, blowing gently, cupping my other hand around the smoke, coaxing and cajoling and finally charming a tiny tongue of yellow flame.

'See! I knew I could do it.'

The ground trembled and I almost fell face-first into my efforts. I didn't want to look up at the volcano. I didn't want to feel the trembling continue on and on and know I had to leave, but I couldn't avoid it. Boiling lava was now being thrown high into the air in great thick clumps, like Cook's morning oatmeal boiling over.

A familiar hooting sound, but louder and urgent. I spun round as Farthing emerged from the hole. I grinned and ran over to her, but something wasn't right. Her scales on one side were blackened and a patch was missing entirely.

I crouched and held out my hand to her. 'Farthing, you're hurt! What happened?'

She ducked back into the gap that led to the lava tube and the cave.

'Let's go back to the mud and put some of it on that wound,' I said, as I followed her.

The lizard waited in the cave and her hoot turned into a growl. Then she ran into the darkness of the tunnel, towards the centre of the island.

Towards the volcano.

CHAPTER TWENTY-SEVEN

I waited. Farthing would come back, she was injured, it didn't—

Another hoot and she reappeared out of the shadows. This time she rose up on her hind legs, ruff flattened against her neck and her hoot was more of a howl, a desperate sound. The hairs rose on my arms.

'What is it, Farthing?'

She darted away but was back within seconds and whine-growling. She pawed the ground.

I shook my head raising my hands. 'I know you want me to follow you again, but the volcano . . .'

The lizard darted forward, grasped the ragged

bottom of my breeches and tugged.

'Hey!'

My trousers were slipping; I'd become thin on a diet of prickly pear. Farthing wouldn't let go, she hauled and jerked and now she was closer I could get a good look at her injuries. The black patch on her side looked like crusted ash, and the skin below it was raw, shiny and bubbling. I'd seen an injury a little like that when Cook had spilt oil on his wrist. Farthing had been scalded. It was like a punch to my chest to see it.

This lizard had survived the dragon fire, yet now she was burnt. I looked closer. Was the wound from . . . lava? Had she been to the erupting volcano?

'Let go, Farthing, please. I don't understand—'

She gave a hard yank, growling, and a piece of fabric tore free. I fell on my back and Farthing sprang on to my chest.

My face was only an inch from her snout. Her copper eyes bored into mine, her claws needled at my ribs. She arched her neck back and her howling whine would have put a wolf to shame.

Something was seriously wrong. Farthing had saved me from the centipede. She'd fed me, found me shelter from the dragon and rescued me from bull sea lions. She might only be a small lizard but if she needed help, I couldn't deny her.

'You win,' I said. 'I'll come and see.'

I stared into the darkness of the tunnel, recalling my panic and the bats. Not in the dark. Not if I could help it.

Avoiding another lunge from Farthing, I scrambled up the rock pile to the surface and ran to the fire, now just a tiny flame.

I looked at the fiddle case. Without it, Scratch would be ruined.

What would your da say?

'I think he'd say I should stay bricky. And do what was right.'

He would say you should help a friend.

I took the old fiddle out of the case, and laid him gently inside the boat. Before I could change my mind, I raised the open case I'd taken such great care with all these years and smashed it down on the rock. It cracked lengthways and, on the second go, into long jagged sticks.

'Sorry, Scratch,' I said, my throat tight. There was no reply. Farthing was waiting at the hole, clawing the ground and growl-whining.

I thrust the end of one long stick into the embers. The old wood had dried in the sun and quickly caught.

With the rest of Scratch's case in the other hand I ran after Farthing once more.

*

The light of my makeshift torch bobbed and flickered as I ran, and I could only just keep Farthing in sight ahead of me in the dark tunnel. I passed the crack in the tunnel roof much more quickly that I would have expected.

At first, I didn't notice it getting warmer. I was already sweating from running and had tied my neckerchief around my forehead to catch the drips before they stung my eyes. The tunnel had taken a downward slope and then a number of turns. I held back. I was sure I'd passed the place where I met the bats last time – where was Farthing taking me? But when she yelped and whined, darting at my trouser legs again, I continued after her.

Suddenly the air became hot and dry, and the heat of it seemed to touch my eyeballs. The floor shook and I careered from side to side, like a drunkard. Was something else happening with the volcano, or did the tremors just feel stronger because I was deep underground? Farthing darted ahead, outside the pool of my torchlight.

'Farthing?'

My voice echoed in a new way, the repeats of my words spaced further apart. Without warning, the tunnel ended.

Ahead of me was a cavern. It was a gigantic bubble in the rock, the size of a cathedral. High above my head was an opening to the surface, the sun streaming down. We must be at the foot of the volcano by now. A wave of heat struck me, along with an unholy stench of fish and rot. I drew my sweat-soaked rag of a kerchief over my nose and mouth and stepped down out of the tunnel in to the epic space, my bare feet crunching painfully on something. I couldn't see Farthing. The floor was thickly covered with some kind of rock, or gravel – jagged, shifting and uneven.

Stumbling on something extra sharp, I looked down at my feet. A skull stared up at me. I recognized the shape of it – a huge fish, maybe a shark. How did it get all the way here? The lava tube didn't flood, or the buccaneer wouldn't be there . . .

There was only one way. I stared up at the patch of sky above.

Farthing had brought me to the dragon's lair.

PART FOUR

All animals feel wonder, and may exhibit curiosity.

CHARLES DARWIN, *THE DESCENT OF MAN*

CHAPTER TWENTY-EIGHT

I stared up at the opening far above me in the roof of the cavern, just wide enough for a dragon.

The light streaming down from it allowed me to look more closely at what I was standing on. I shuddered. A carpet of bones. Mostly small – fish, I guessed – some encased in large round dried-out droppings. I could see no sign of anything that looked . . . human. But it would be difficult to tell. I picked up the largest bone I could see, it looked like the jaw of a small whale.

What would Mr Darwin make of it? He found it fascinating to dissect animal droppings to find out which animal they belonged to and what they'd been eating, and these were as big as a human skull.

Which was about right, considering the size of the animal that lived here.

My heart fluttered in my throat and the sweat soaked through my kerchief and dripped in my eyes. I scanned the cavern for Farthing.

When she hooted, the sound echoed on and on, like we were inside a gigantic hollow ball. I finally spotted her, a flash of green on a wide ledge that jutted from the cavern wall. I didn't rightly know what to do. I'd been trying to avoid the dragon since I was washed up here and Farthing had seemed to understand that very well, so why had she led me right to it? Ever since I'd met her, she'd helped me – fed me, defended me – or had I imagined that?

'Come on, Farthing, we can't be here,' I hissed.

She whined, and the high pitch sound echoed. I imagined it spiralling around the walls and out of the opening way above me, alerting the cave's owner.

I shuddered as I crushed across the bones and droppings. Farthing ducked back on the ledge out of sight. This was no time for playing; she couldn't have brought me here for that. I propped my burning torch up against the cave wall.

'What are you *doing* up there?'

The cave shook, and the layer of bones jangled until

they covered my feet; it was like being inside an immense baby's rattle. This time the tremors continued, on and on, and the heat grew unbearable. I needed to run for it, now.

I made up my mind; I was taking Farthing with me. I wasn't leaving her here in a volcanic eruption, and I didn't care if she bit or scratched me. I reached out over the ledge, which was just higher than my head, and felt a scattering of rocks, dried seaweed and something soft and bouncy, like moss.

Then my fingers found the curve of a smooth, warm surface.

I rolled the object towards me. Farthing appeared and nudged it off the edge, and I caught it in both my waiting hands.

It was golden, shot through with marbled lines of black.

I had known what it was the moment I'd touched that perfect roundness, but I hadn't wanted to believe it.

A dragon's egg.

CHAPTER TWENTY-NINE

I held the golden egg tight to my chest, suddenly afraid I would drop it, and stared up at the hole in the cavern way above me.

I remembered Mr Darwin's excitement at the huge rhea eggs we'd found on the mud banks in Patagonia; this was half that size again. The biggest egg ever found. Just one of these golden eggs would be a wonder of the world. Mr Darwin only ever took what we needed, he was very particular about that, especially when it came to birds' nests. Yet Farthing was nudging more eggs forward along the ledge. Six, now seven.

My thoughts were interrupted by a screech that made

the contents of the cave jangle and clatter, and a burning wind buffeted my back. I spun round, as the dragon's two huge claws descended through the roof of the cavern.

I hooked one hand under Farthing's belly and slung her across my shoulder, she was lighter than I would have thought and curled herself around my neck. With my other arm cradling the egg, I ran from the cavern, ducking into the entrance tunnel. A second screech rocked me to my core, and I clutched my ear with my free hand, crouching in the dark, out of the dragon's sight.

A different sound tore the air, like old sheets being ripped up for bandages. The earth beneath my feet didn't tremble this time; it slid back and forth like a heavy load on rollers. I collapsed to the ground, clasping the egg. With Farthing still wrapped around my neck, I squeezed my eyes tight, waiting for the entire tunnel to collapse on my head.

The rumble died away, leaving the air swirling with dust and stinking as if the guts of the earth had split open. I pressed my neckerchief over my nose and peered into the cavern.

The dragon filled the cave with muscular golden bulk. She nudged at the ledge with her huge snout, pushing the eggs back. All the while she was groaning and rumbling, a sound not unlike the earthquakes, her huge sides panting like bellows. Up close she was beyond magnificent. Her folded wings were a deeper bronze than her scales, which glittered gold where the light hit. She was bigger than ten elephants, maybe bigger than a whale.

Her head whipped towards me, and I pressed my back against the wall, in the shadow of the tunnel.

She sniffed the air through cavernous nostrils on the end of a majestic, long snout. Her dinner plate eyes opened wide and were mesmerizing, a burnished gold like her scales. She reared and bellowed again, a teeth-jangling tormented shriek. Now I saw the reason for her horror.

Red-orange glowing clots of lava were dropping from the hole above. As the molten rock splatted into the scree of the cave it sizzled, and the fish carcasses and dung released choking black smoke.

The dragon had chosen a place near the volcano – perhaps even at its base – for her nest, so heat couldn't be harmful to her eggs, maybe it was even good for them. But the lava would surely kill them; it had to be why Farthing had nudged the eggs towards me. And why had the little lizard wanted to rescue her enemy's eggs? She had wanted to rescue me too, and I supposed that didn't make sense either. Maybe the lizard and the dragon were connected, like the birds that pecked lice from the tortoises' necks. There wasn't time to consider it, I needed to escape; the lava was now pouring into the cave in continuous lumps like milk curds.

The volcano had erupted.

CHAPTER THIRTY

I watched from the entrance of the tunnel, crouched, still clutching a dragon egg, warm against my chest. Avoiding the smoking pool of lava now in the centre of the cavern, the dragon turned to the ledge so she was almost facing my hiding place, but she didn't seem interested in me. She tried to take an egg in her mouth, but her jaws were too huge, her teeth too sharp, and she nudged it right off the ledge and into the bones below. She nosed at it again, her massive claws tensing, crunching the scree beneath them. I inhaled sharply then coughed in the smoke, then froze. Had the giant beast heard me? Farthing sprung from around my neck, but I caught hold of the base of her tail and hauled her back as the dragon roared, spurting two streams of fire from her nostrils up into the cavern above. She had to be the most powerful creature on earth, but she couldn't save her eggs. I should be running for my life ... but my heart was squeezed tight by her anguish.

I'd known that feeling. I'd known that feeling in the times I'd tried to forget, when Da had writhed in fever and cried for Ma, and there was nothing I could do to stop him joining her. I'd felt like shrieking up at the heavens too.

When the dragon unfurled her wings, an almighty dollop of lava engulfed her. She tried to shake free; and in a spray of burning droplets her head and body emerged. She didn't seem to have been burnt by it, though goodness knows, the heat must have been more than a blacksmith's forge. I couldn't make out what she was doing – snapping and clawing at the lava ...

One outstretched wing was now pinned by the weight of the molten rock.

The dragon was trapped.

I watched in horror as she struggled to release herself and screeched, sending more plumes of fire into the air. Farthing darted free of my grip and scampered up the curved wall and on to the ledge.

I couldn't leave the eggs to be swallowed by lava. The

only dragon eggs in the world, gone, and their mother with them. My decision, a wild unthinking decision, was made, and I didn't have long. What would I carry them in? I only had the shirt on my back.

Then the shirt on my back would do.

I stripped it off and crunched as lightly as I could across the bones to the ledge, the lava now only a couple of yards away. The dragon was distracted, turned away from me, using her snout and claws to try to work her wing out of the heavy lava, flicking great clumps of it into the air. I tied the arms of the shirt together, and looped it around my torso and over my shoulder to make a sling.

Farthing nudged the golden eggs down into it, as the dragon roared in agony and torment.

Shivers ran over my neck, spine and behind my knees, in dreadful expectation of dragon fire engulfing me at any second. It didn't come. I counted seven eggs into the fabric, and they clicked together like strong china, the shells rigid and hot against my chest.

Farthing leapt down, and we raced from the cave. I stopped to snatch up the first egg from the mouth of the tunnel and added it to the others, then looked back to see the dragon, coated in great clots of molten orange rock, only one wing free and flapping . . . frantic. As we left, she screamed – a racket so loud, and higher and higher in pitch. I collapsed against the tunnel wall as the unearthly shriek pickaxed through my skull. Too loud, it was too loud. My ear seemed to swell, and then the sound was only on one side of my head as the other side exploded in agony.

CHAPTER THIRTY-ONE

The dragon's scream tailed off, but my injured ear beat like a gong, and I staggered, unbalanced, as Farthing raced ahead down the lava tube, away from the cavern. I didn't have time to worry about the damage to my ear, I was running for my life. Smoke stung my eyes and the fabric of my sweat-soaked neckerchief sucked at my mouth, but I daren't move it for fear the stench would choke me. There was a sharp pain in my foot, not the centipede sting but a new hurt, since walking barefoot on the bones of the cave. I couldn't let that slow me either. The eight huge eggs were heavy across my chest, like the sacks of potatoes my aunt had made me haul from the market. I risked a glance behind me. The flow of the lava had turned into a flood of molten rock, now pouring into the tunnel, crackling and hissing, its fumes and heat racing ahead of it.

The mother dragon was alive when we left her but must have drowned in this boiling rock by now. Did she see me take the eggs, or think they had died with her? I didn't have time for pity. If I stopped or tripped, I'd be going the same way. The lava surged and bubbled, spattering the back of my legs with scalding flecks. If I'd reached the hole in the tunnel ceiling any later I would have been done for.

Lava was dripping through from the surface here too.

The flow had chased me both above and below ground. I dodged around it, the rocks hot beneath my feet. This new stream of lava would join what was behind me, and it was only going to get faster. The eggs clanked and Farthing scuttled ahead.

What exactly happens to a person engulfed by molten rock?

Probably not the best moment to think about that.

There would be nothing left. Not even bones for even an intrepid scientist like Mr Darwin to dig from the rock. No one was going to find my ashy remains and send me home to London for men to talk about over their fancy cigars.

I wasn't going to let this hellhole be my tomb.

Light ahead. Not the eerie red of the lava, but the pure light of sun. I raced through the buccaneer's cave and ducked out, on to the earth's surface where I belonged, and pulled down my neckerchief to heave in gulps of fresh air.

There was no time to rest. The volcano was in full furious eruption, spraying out its molten insides. Above me flew a flock of the huge pink birds. Great hunks of red lava flew into the air like a giant infant flinging sand, and more flooded from the summit, a river slowly engulfing the plain. The flows advanced towards me from two directions, merging with each other in a thick burning tide. Ahead of it skittered a retreating army of red Sally Lightfoot crabs.

Despite my exhaustion, my feet raced across the black mud to the boat. I threw the chest in, flung it open, stepped out of the makeshift sling and tumbled the eggs inside, still bundled in my shirt. I would leave, as I was, shirtless and barefoot, with a broken oar, a copper pan, a knife and my fiddle without a case.

The sea was calm . . . but the island was raging.

CHAPTER THIRTY-TWO

Farthing. Where was she?

'Farthing!' I screamed. I couldn't remember when I'd last seen her. She was in front of me as I climbed from the cave, I was sure of it.

'Farthing!'

I grabbed the rope I had tied to the prow of the rowboat and pulled. On the second tug the boat *slooped* out of the mud, and on the third tug the hull started to slide. It gained momentum until I was almost running. The lava made its journey across the jagged rocks, empty of the iguanas I'd always seen draped there.

'Farthing!'

It wasn't much further to the sea, and I forced my trembling muscles on. The water lapped wonderfully cool around my ankles then my thighs, stinging as it hit the burns from the spitting lava, and the boat lifted. I tipped myself in, as three thick tongues of lava hit the wet mudflats, sizzling and sending up huge plumes of steam.

I searched the shoreline for a glimpse of green. I couldn't be sure of the last time I'd seen her. Had she fallen behind, been engulfed by the lava, and I hadn't even noticed?

No. The little lizard had survived the dragon fire before, she must have escaped again. She'd be sheltering somewhere safe from the lava, somewhere I couldn't go.

I couldn't wait for her. I couldn't stay here any longer. I looked down at the chest. The dragon eggs were my responsibility. They might be the last of their kind in the world, and Farthing had brought me to their mother's lair to rescue them. And with or without Farthing, I had to keep them safe.

I used the oar to direct me out to sea, and once I was past the small breakers I stopped to wait. A wall of black smoke and ash billowed towards me.

I willed Farthing to appear. Please, just this one thing.

If you wait any longer, this will all have been for nothing.

'I know. I know.'

I looked at my fiddle and cleared my raw throat.

There were only a few tiny spurts of water along the seams of the boat, my rosin wax treatment had worked better than I could have imagined, but there was no way to keep Scratch dry now. I could lay the fiddle on top of the eggs in the chest, but the neck would stick out and I wouldn't be able to close it. If we were hit by a wave the fiddle and eggs would both tumble out.

Farthing risked her life to stop the eggs being engulfed in lava. As long as I was alive, I'd keep them safe for her.

I cleared my throat and ran my hand over my da's old fiddle.

'Thank you for all the songs, old friend. I'm —'

Concentrate on your rowing. Promise me that, sonny Syms.

Sonny Syms. That was what *Da* used to call me.

'Da?'

Scratch and Da.

My Da . . . and Scratch.

A snatch of a distant sea shanty rang in my pulsing ear.

I took a breath and coughed soot from my lungs. I felt a painful release in my ear, but still no sound. I touched it and my fingers came away slicked with blood.

The volcano now shot almighty gouts of molten rock

high into the air, erupting in horrifying splendour. More black smoke mushroomed from its summit, following me out to sea like the worst London pea-souper. The eggy chemical stench was dizzying and, for all I knew, it could kill me.

I closed the chest, and rowed for my life.

CHAPTER THIRTY-THREE

I knelt in the bottom of the tiny boat, shirtless and coated in ash – blistered and raw, parched and starved – and heaved my oar through the water on one side then the other, then bailed, rowed and bailed, my back bared to the beating sun. I didn't dare stop, as the stinking black cloud chased me out to sea. Ground-shaking rumbles of the volcano created giant ripples that clashed with the waves, splashing me. My fiddle was already ruined. Scratch watched me, and as the water swilled around his base I felt my heart was drowning too. The last thing there was left of my da.

Not the last thing. You're what's left. And you're still

here. Stay bricky.

I forced a smile. It was the last I ever heard from Scratch, as the fiddle slipped to the side of the chest and was waterlogged in the growing pool at the bottom of the boat.

Da, gone.

Mr Darwin and my crewmates, gone.

Farthing, gone.

And now Scratch, gone too.

The breeze picked up, and the smoke thinned and was whipped away in swirls. The island was death, but when I surveyed the empty mass of water ahead of me, I shuddered with the fear of a boy who knows the sea all too well. A boy who knows the empty ocean has been deadly for thousands more men than any volcano eruption.

Or dragon.

I tried to recall Mr Darwin's Galapagos map. It showed a cluster of islands together, Narborough wasn't far from Albemarle. But maps were always a lie. The islands were not easy to travel between, not for one desperate boy in a tiny boat. I lost myself in the effort of rowing and bailing until I was surrounded by nothing but water, the blotch of smoke on the horizon all I could see of the island I'd escaped. I almost wanted to row back now, just to have sight of land!

I strained at the oar trying not to think at all, until darting lights appeared before my eyes and the tremble in my arms made it impossible to continue.

I flopped back, leaning on the chest to rest, clutching my twitching arm muscles. Nothing but water in any direction. The wind was brisk and the sea calm, and this gave me the tiniest reason to hope. There was good visibility and it was the kind of day that the *Beagle* would be at sail. Maybe they knew where I was yet had been unable to get to me, and now with the volcano erupting they would come. I knew in my deepest heart this hope was a liar, but I tried to listen to it all the same.

The sky was a deadly hot blue, adding blisters to my lava scalds. I should open the chest to find my shirt, wet it and cover my head. Thirst was now my biggest enemy.

A shadow passed over me. I opened my eyes. A shadow swooping, low and close, a shadow with wing tips skimming the water.

She had escaped the lava. I couldn't think how.

She was golden and glorious and petrifying. Thirst was *not* my biggest enemy.

This was a dragon mother, and she was searching for her eggs.

CHAPTER THIRTY-FOUR

I cowered low in the base of the boat, water sloshing around me. The dragon had neither burnt nor devoured me when she dropped me repeatedly into the sea on that first day. Her behaviour was a warning. She was brooding her eggs, and visitors were not welcome. And now her eggs were in the chest by my head. She circled the boat.

Did this mother understand that they would have been engulfed by the lava – that I had saved them?

Her shriek drowned my thoughts, and I yelped with the pain from my injured ear. The wind of her wings battered me, rocking the boat. I was like a sacrifice offered up to a mythical beast, completely helpless.

Should I reveal to her what was in the chest? Maybe she could scoop up the eggs in her mouth and save them after all. I could return them to her.

But if she were able to carry the eggs, then she would have done so in the cavern.

With a grinding shriek the dragon released a stream of fire.

It smashed into the sea to my side, shooting up plumes of steam. I curled up, folding myself as small as possible.

All was quiet.

The wind of her wings eased. When I dared to crane my head upwards, she was almost directly above me and staring down like an avenging angel or devil, her body in a tightly controlled hover I recognized from watching a hawk about to dive on its prey.

My survival instinct took over. The ancient knife, blackened with age, was in the base of the boat. I grasped it, a tiny weapon less than a tenth the size of one of the dragon's claws, but something is always better than nothing. I would stand and fight. I balanced in the boat, water swilling at my ankles, watching her plummet. She knew the eggs were in the chest, I was sure of it.

I remembered her screams of anguish in the cavern.

I couldn't attack her, I just . . . couldn't. I threw the knife aside.

I grabbed the chest and leant heavily to the side, capsizing the entire boat and tipping myself into the sea, the boat over my head. I lost hold of the chest. The slats covered me like a roof, and when the dragon fire hit the wet wood, it did not catch at first. But with a second shrieking blast the fire took hold and I was in a tiny cave of flame. I ducked down beneath the sea, chunks of the boat floated ablaze above me, blocking my route to air. I kicked away as hard as I could, underwater, until my lungs were bursting and I was forced to surface.

I gasped and sputtered, spinning, scanning the sky all around me. Empty.

The last scraps of the ancient boat smouldered, and sank.

CHAPTER THIRTY-FIVE

Something dark bobbed on the surface of the water. At first I imagined it was my fiddle, somehow making it all this way to join me, just like when I first dragged it from the surf. But it was the wooden treasure chest.

I splashed over to it, grappled at the damp slippery wood, singed and blackened but still strong, then rested my head and arms over the chest and let it hold me up.

The dragon did not return.

Now I would just wait for the sharks to snap at my drifting legs. Or the sun, or a delirium that made me drink seawater, or drowning. There were a lot of ways to die out here, everything hurt and I'd run out of ideas.

I do not know how long I floated, head and arms draped over the chest. I thought I'd been in trouble before, but it was a trifle compared to being adrift. My thirst became an agonizing torment that controlled both my body and mind, but it also prevented me from sleeping so deeply that I would let go of the wooden trunk, which was the only thing keeping me afloat. My arms weakened and I repeatedly slipped, almost losing the chest, but each time my body clung to it, without the help of my mind. I hallucinated, though not like the poison dreams after the centipede bite. My mind saw islands, trees growing in the middle of the ocean, boats . . . I was carried up and down waves of hope followed by crushing disappointment.

I pressed my chin against the wood and imagined it was my fiddle; I fingered ballads, shanties and jigs to the sun and the sea, humming in the back of my cracked throat, trying to chase away the torture of thirst with the memory of songs. I sobbed a little then, but my body was so dry that no tears fell.

Finally, at night, I fell from my chest raft completely and woke, spluttering, some yards from it. I somehow found new strength to release my ragged trousers and use them to tie myself around the chest. The eggs and I would die together in the ocean, me in only my torn undergarments. I managed a smile at the thought, then groaned in pain when my parched lips split open. I'd exhausted myself and fell asleep, cheek pressed against the wood as it had once pressed against Scratch's case.

I awoke to a nudge at the wooden chest. And another. The floating trunk was being bumped by something, pushing us along.

Sharks. It had to be. I'd thought things couldn't get worse, but I'd been wrong. I groaned. Of all the ways to die . . .

I couldn't even open my eyes. I reached my hands over and splashed some water on my face to loosen the salt crust that gummed my eyelids shut.

I blinked. It was another vision.

Two glowing copper farthings. A triangular green snout.

I didn't want to reach out a hand because she would surely disappear. I just drank her in with my eyes.

'Farthing.' The sound that emerged from my mouth was eerie, a hoarse whisper, and if I'd had any tears, they would have stung my burnt and blistered face. When my sobs turned to a laugh, I groaned with the pain in my throat.

The lizard had to be a cruel illusion. But she was a stubborn one. And she was nudging at the chest, rocking it, pushing it. I reached out my trembling hand and she nudged it with her snout, firm and smooth, a hot breath on my palm.

Farthing had found me.

If this weren't real, I would gladly go along with it.

She butted the chest powerfully and I stared into her eyes as she swam, her limbs paddling and her stumpy injured tail whipping from side to side. It was sunrise. I felt like she and I were the only beings alive.

I would not die alone. And although the thirst torture continued, every time I looked at Farthing, I could bear it.

Voices. I did not bother to lift my head – it must be more waking dreams. But they were male voices . . . and familiar.

'Ahoy! Man in the water!'

'You there, show us you can hear us.'

'I think the poor fellow has heard his last.'

'What is that pushing him? A sea lion?'

I raised my heavy head from the wood.

'By blazes, it's the lad!'

'Covington!'

Farthing stopped paddling and sank down in the water so only her eyes and the nostrils on her snout were visible. Our eyes met. She snorted, swimming forward a little, and I reached out and laid my fingers on her jaw. Her scales were smooth and warmer than the water that surrounded us. I raised my head.

There was a ship.

The *Beagle*. I blinked, and it didn't blur, float or vanish. It *was* the *Beagle*. And, closer than that, a rowboat.

I turned back to Farthing and she lifted her front claws up on to the chest.

'Come with me,' I whispered. 'There's nothing there for you now.'

I wrapped my arm around her and pressed my forehead against her smooth scales. Strong arms hauled us out of the ocean, together.

CHAPTER THIRTY-SIX

'By Jove, 'tis the boy, Covington,' said a voice I recognized. Robbins. I gasped a sob of relief as his strong arms lifted me on deck, and a rough hand remained on my shoulder.

'You're alright now, lad.'

More voices. I couldn't make sense of what they were saying.

I scratched my fingers against the hard wood of the hull. The *Beagle*. I was really saved. 'Farth . . . Farthing. Where . . .'

'Is he talking about the lizard?'

'Get a hold of it, then.'

'Ouch! You little . . .'

'Wrap the blighter in a sack, Mr Darwin will want a look . . .'

I was sliced free of the chest, yet I clung to it. They gave up trying to separate me from it. When I flailed and hit out at them, they hauled me out of the rowboat and on to the dry deck, taking the wooden chest with me. Billows of black, like the volcanic smoke, closed in behind my eyes as I was overwhelmed by exhaustion and relief but . . . Farthing.

A hoot from somewhere close by. She was here, safe. I pressed my face against the hot dry deck and let the dark clouds close in.

'Covington, can you hear me?' The voice grew louder. 'He's coming round, fetch Mr Bynoe and Mr Darwin, quick smart.'

'Covington, my dear, dear boy,' Mr Darwin's voice brought me to my senses. Sound was muffled in one ear, loud in the other. I turned to hear him better and everything hurt. My young master. Alive. He slid a hand beneath my head and held a cup to my lips. I recognized I was in the territory of Mr Bynoe, the ship's surgeon, the low cabin of sickbay, lined with narrow cots.

I shook my head, sending the cabin spinning. 'Farthing . . .'

'The lizard is right here, Covington, perfectly healthy. You wouldn't settle until it was by your side.'

Mr Darwin lifted a small crate with slats at the front, through which I could see a flicker of green, a disc of copper. I reached out, but hardly had the strength to lift my arm. Farthing wouldn't like being confined in there. When she hoot-growled at me, a lump filled my throat. She was safe, which was all that mattered right now.

'She's a new species, boy, and quite unique. I'm calling her the Galapagos green lizard.'

The master offered me the water again and I sipped, and found it both sweet and salty with a bitter edge. So, so good. When I attempted to gulp, it ran down my chin. I spluttered and Mr Darwin wiped my mouth with his handkerchief. To see those intelligent blue-grey eyes, the bushy eyebrows high, so serious and concerned over me, gave me a nasty shock. I was the servant here – I tended Mr Darwin when he was sickened by heavy seas, and that was how it should be. This felt all wrong.

'Don't trouble—' it came out as barely a rough whisper.

'Nonsense, boy. You've had rather a rough time of it.' He leant in closer. 'You saved my life, Covington. I have told everyone. We didn't expect . . . We saw the eruption on Narborough.'

I slurped at the drink and the clouds in my mind parted. So the island *was* Narborough and the volcano had brought them to me.

'The eggs? The dragon eggs?'

Mr Darwin chuckled, and that familiar light appeared in his eyes. His side whiskers had merged into a new growth of beard, he couldn't have shaved since I last saw him.

'Rather unique specimens, I do agree. How clever of you to retrieve them despite your ordeal, although I dare say you would not have survived without the watertight chest to act as a buoy. Did you happen to see the bird that laid them? I am imagining a giant ground grouse, or was it some form of greater Galapagos penguin . . . forgive me, dear boy, you must not even think of it until you are more yourself.'

He dabbed at my forehead with a damp cloth as I stared up at him. I raised myself on my elbows.

'It was . . . a *dragon*.' I whispered.

CHAPTER THIRTY-SEVEN

Mr Darwin smiled again, but concern crumpled the corners of his eyes. 'Bynoe says you were frightfully battered and may easily have a concussion. Your eardrum is perforated, you've suffered the effects of exposure, and the toxic gases released by the volcano may have caused—'

'No!' I surprised myself with the sudden strength in my voice. 'There *was* a dragon. I found her nest. Those are the dragon's eggs.'

I shocked myself at my rudeness, speaking to my master in this way, but Mr Darwin laid a gentle hand on my shoulder. I was bandaged there. I realized I was bandaged almost everywhere. The burns.

'When you were in the throes of delirium, you would not be quieted until I had the chest brought in here alongside the lizard. The eggs are still inside.'

He crossed to the other side of the sickbay and lifted the chest lid. I caught a golden glint.

'I told Mr Bynoe and the seamen not to lay a hand on it, and Fitzroy will not interfere. If my boy saviour wants to take a special interest in some rare specimens, then the least I can do is grant this wish.' He leant closer, and softened his tone. 'You do realize that the eggs will not survive, dear boy. We have had no success with bringing back live egg specimens. Depending on its diet, the lizard may fare better.'

Bring the eggs *back*?

Eight dragon eggs. Most likely the only dragon eggs in the world. If they didn't survive the trip . . .

'No. They belong here. In the Galapagos.'

Mr Darwin scratched his whiskers and gave a little shake of his head, pouches of worry forming beneath his eyes.

'We would be better off blowing them or preserving them, then at least they won't spoil . . .' He swallowed and looked away. He wanted to make a hole in the eggs and blow out the contents – or, if there were young inside, they would . . .

'No!' My broken voice was shrill, as I struggled to sit upright. 'Please . . . sir. No . . .'

Mr Darwin pressed my shoulders gently, so I lay back on the pillow.

'Covington. Mr Bynoe said strictly no excitement. You must rest now. I will not touch the eggs, or the lizard. You have my word on it.'

My eyelids were too heavy, my voice slurring. He was right about eggs not surviving – there had to be another way. Another place where they would have a chance. Maybe they were close to hatching.

'They can't die . . . they are the only . . . leave them on Alber . . . marle,' I gasped. 'In a . . . cave . . .'

My throat seized up and I sipped more water, now feeling as though I might vomit it back up.

'I am sorry, dear boy, believe me. But the Galapagos are now some five hundred miles behind us. Our next stop is Polynesia, over four thousand miles distant.'

My mouth dropped open in horror. Even in my state of exhaustion, I needed to gather myself enough to make him believe me. I cleared my throat, wincing.

'It was a dragon, on my life, I swear. A miracle. Bigger . . . than a whale, with scales, and reptile in shape. Four legs, leathery wings which were huge beyond belief . . . I was not delirious, sir, I swear it . . .'

My hoarse whisper died off and I managed to hold

the cup myself, although my head felt as if it might float clear off my body. Mr Darwin observed me like a new specimen. If the young scientist wanted to make a name for himself, he had to understand that this would be the find of his life and would surely make him world famous.

'You always tell me, sir, open eyes, open mind. The huge fossil skull you found . . . one of those ancient giants, sir, but alive, very . . . alive . . . a dragon. If the eggs die . . .'

My voice slurred and my eyelids drooped. I tried to blink them open and failed.

A dragging sound, and then Mr Darwin laid my hand upon the dry wood of the chest he had placed beside my cot.

Exhaustion overtook me so utterly that I wondered what the surgeon had put in that water.

CHAPTER THIRTY-EIGHT

When I next awoke, Mr Darwin produced a bowl of bone broth which the ship's cook, Phillips, had made especially for me. My mouth watered at the savoury smell. But first I checked on Farthing's crate. I could only make out a dash of green through the slats. I needed to get her out.

'Has she had food? Water? Sir?' I asked.

'She has,' said Mr Darwin. 'She eats all types of fish, bones and all. She's not particular.'

I stole glances at Mr Darwin's face as he helped me sip the broth. My stomach settled and the cabin no longer spun. Something had changed between us – the rules of servant and master didn't fit as easily as they used to.

'Farthing was wounded, sir. I would like to check on her. She is not dangerous . . . please, sir.'

Mr Darwin frowned. 'You mean release her into sickbay? I do not think Mr Bynoe or Captain—'

'There's no one here, and they wouldn't need to know, sir,' I said quickly, and then flushed. I was interrupting, and my request was bold.

Mr Darwin stood, and I expected him to snatch the crate up and remove Farthing, but he crossed the cabin and pushed the door closed, shaking his head. Then he helped me sit up on the edge of the bunk. I was shaky but felt much better.

The young gentleman slid aside the front of the crate and adjusted his stool further back as he peered in. Farthing was curled in shadow at the back of the crate.

Nobody moved. I slid to the floor, sitting cross-legged in my nightshirt before her.

'Farthing. You're safe here.'

The lizard flicked her tail, and after a few seconds she moved towards me. I held out my hand and she butted it with her snout and gave a soft hoot. I grinned and although I could not take my gaze from Farthing, out of the corner of my eye, I saw Mr Darwin lean forward to look closer. Her green scales seemed almost iridescent against the dull browns of the cabin and the crate, and her eyes caught the lamplight with a flash of new copper.

'Now I see why you called her Farthing,' whispered Mr Darwin.

I nodded. Farthing ventured out of the crate completely and turned to survey the room, remaining close to me. The ruff of scales was flat against her neck and I could see she was scared, but at least the wounds on her tail and side were crusted over.

'She seems in good condition,' said Mr Darwin.

He spoke softly, shadows falling long on his face by the light of the storm lamp.

Farthing sniffed the air. She stalked over to the door and snuffled at the base of it, then continued to investigate all the corners of the tiny cabin. Mr Darwin and I simply watched her.

I returned to the bed, the effort of sitting on the hard floor making me suddenly dizzy. When I laid back, Farthing jumped up by my side and rested her head on her foreclaws.

'Remarkable,' said Mr Darwin. I nodded. 'The shape of its scales, and that colouring; quite unique for the reptiles of the islands. Sap green? I shall have to consult Werner.'

'I thought pistachio green, sir.'

Our eyes met and we both smiled just a little.

'Quite right. But we can't have it – her – roaming . . .'

'Just for a little while, sir? She saved my life. More than once.'

Silence. Just the creak of the boat timber, rope against cleats, the snap of the sail. Farthing saved my life and I saved Mr Darwin's.

He cleared his throat, his eyes flicking between the lizard and me.

'Ah yes, about the storm. You have had a remarkable experience, my good fellow,' he paused, and I couldn't meet his eyes. Mr Darwin had never called me that before.

'I would dearly like to hear everything. From the moment we lost hold of each other in the squall. If you are ready to tell it.'

I smiled and reached for water. With Farthing beside me, I was ready.

CHAPTER THIRTY-NINE

I told Mr Darwin everything, the truth in all its burning impossible detail. Throughout the long tale, my master stroked his whiskers and watched me with those sharp, thoughtful eyes. He did not interrupt and didn't take notes. I stammered a little – despite all the long days we spent together I'd never really spoken about myself – but was determined to tell it all. I even included my conversations with Scratch. The telling made it real again.

When I finished, my cheeks burning, breathless, Mr Darwin made me sip water. He waited for me to settle and then held something beneath the lamp. It glinted gold.

'While you were sleeping, Mr Bynoe removed this nasty article from the sole of your foot, dear boy. Quite a splinter. It suggests at least one of the eggs you mention had . . . already hatched?'

I held out my hand and he dropped the shard of shell into it. It was a triangular curled sliver, as long as my thumbnail and almost as wide at the base. Gold struck through with black on the outer side, pale and pearly on the inside. Thin, but very hard. Already *hatched*?

I didn't need to look at the dragon eggs to know it was from an egg like them.

'I checked all the eggs myself,' said Mr Darwin. 'None are cracked.'

Farthing had nudged each egg into my arms. There couldn't have been a newly hatched infant up there on the ledge too. Could there?

I imagined a miniature golden dragon. It might be helpless and blind like a baby bird, fallen from the ledge into the bones, unseen, as the lava filled the cave. I shivered. The mother dragon survived so maybe she had already rescued it when she found me at sea.

Mr Darwin sighed deeply and rubbed his shock of wispy hair. 'I will think on this long and hard, Covington, you have my word. But I cannot imagine the anatomy of an animal with four legs and then two extra limbs – the wings you describe. There is no animal with this physiology, it is simply not possible. And for a creature of that magnitude to lift itself off the ground and fly . . . it is against the laws of physics, dear boy.'

I sunk back on to the pillows. 'You don't believe me, but it's the truth, sir.'

'I know *you* believe that. There is no shame in these imaginings, after the ordeal you have been through. No shame at all.'

Mr Darwin would not believe me because he *could* not believe me. It was not his fault; I hadn't believed it myself at first, when I thought it was a sky beast that had swept me into the air. Dragons just weren't believable.

'Now then. When you are feeling stronger, Bynoe advises you spend some time on deck. Your only duty is to make a full recovery. But I think keep . . . aspects . . . of your experience on Narborough Island between you and me. By all means share your adventure with the crew, but possibly omit the parts about . . .'

'The dragon,' I said.

Mr Darwin nodded. I saw the sense in what he said. Being known as the poor boy who left his senses on a Galapagos island wasn't going to help me. I needed to protect Farthing and those eggs.

I reached out to the chest beside my cot and Farthing

butted my wrist.

The dragon's eggs were safe. At that moment, I chose to believe they would hatch. And when they did, everyone would see the truth for themselves.

PART FIVE

*. . . love for all living creatures, the most
noble attribute of man.*

CHARLES DARWIN, *THE DESCENT OF MAN*

CHAPTER FORTY

The next stop on our voyage was the Polynesian island of Tahiti, where green mountains rose out of lagoons of turquoise glass, surrounded by coral reefs. I was strong enough to go ashore and insisted Farthing come with me. The people were some of the friendliest we had met and paid little mind to the green lizard following me around. We stocked up on both meat and fruit. The sweet bananas made a welcome change, after a month of eating only the fish we caught and Cook Phillips' lobscouse. Lobscouse was midday rations – made with potato, onion, salt pork and a pound of ship's biscuit to soak it up.

New Zealand was different again. Mr Darwin was impressed with the tree ferns but disappointed by the lack of animals. We were all impatient to leave. Maybe a lot of the sailors were keen to be back on English soil, but I wasn't one of them. I had all I needed right there on board.

When the call for 'Land ho!' came again, I gathered at the ship's rails next to Mr Darwin, although without the telescope there was nothing to see yet. A tug on my breeches' leg. I crouched and rested an arm on deck so Farthing could scamper the length of it and settle across my shoulders like a giant stole. She rarely did this, but I liked it when she did, although I was sure she was getting heavier than she used to be. It had now been a month since I'd been rescued.

I looked along the row of officers which Mr Darwin had insisted I join. I'd been spending more time with them than the men. Without my fiddle, I had little reason to be in the sailors' mess, and Mr Darwin kept me busy at work in the captain's cabin, preparing the specimens, labelling, logging and sketching. Mr Bynoe had been impressed with how quickly I had recovered from my Galapagos ordeal, both in body and mind, although my ear would never be right again; I had almost totally lost my hearing on that side. At first it had made my walking wobbly, but I had already grown used to it. Mr Bynoe had been confused by this injury.

'The eardrum looks to be ruptured. How did this happen?' he'd said, after peering into my ear through a funnel shaped instrument.

'A very loud noise, sir,' I said. I had looked to Mr Darwin who stood behind him, and he shook his head.

'Hmm. I have never seen the like. And what made this noise?'

I blinked and glanced at Mr Darwin. 'The . . . volcano, sir,' I said.

Both men were silent.

'An infection is a more probable cause,' said Mr Bynoe, packing his case. My master's headshake turned into a nod.

I took Mr Darwin's advice, kept my thoughts and memories of the dragon locked away, like the eggs inside the chest.

My behaviour towards the eggs and Farthing gave Captain Fitzroy 'cause for concern' – he likely thought me addled in the mind and Mr Darwin addled for indulging me – but it couldn't be helped. To find a boy presumed lost at sea, still alive after six days, was good luck for the ship, and the sailors tipped their caps at me. In general, we sailors were a fanciful lot and some even touched my shoulder and muttered – clutching at crucifixes and lucky charms, hoping my fortune would pass their way. The first time Farthing escaped the cabin, I had been awful feared she would leap from the rail and swim for home, or a sailor would take violent to her. It did not happen. In only a few days, the crew, and even the captain, accepted Farthing's wanderings on deck. She never damaged anything, and her inquisitive nature and playfulness made the men laugh. She even won the heart of her rival, the ship's cat; when Farthing caught rats, she delivered them to the big lazy ginger tom for him to devour. Farthing never ate a rat herself, much preferring the fish we caught, especially crabs and lobster, which she crunched up, shell and all.

I finally persuaded Mr Darwin to put me back on light deck duties as well as working with him in his cabin, and my body grew strong again. Farthing took to climbing the boom of the mainsail, basking in the Pacific sun. Even the sailors working aloft – who thought themselves a class above – didn't mind her. She watched me from on high as I worked. At night, she could be coaxed back in her crate and even seemed to become used to it. Yes, it had been a strange month all right.

Mr Darwin broke through my thoughts.

'Quite a picture. I've heard it is every bit as agreeable as it looks.'

Ahead of us spread Sydney harbour. The sun glittered

bright on the water of the marina and the soft hills rising behind them were pale green. Even at a distance, the town seemed orderly and well-spaced, sheltered from the sea by the natural shape of the cove.

'Covington, are you ready? I plan to take you ashore with me right away. Farthing will need to stay aboard without you for a short while.'

I opened my mouth and closed it again. Mr Darwin knew I didn't like to confine her. He turned to me and smiled, eyes flashing beneath his brows.

'Trust me, good fellow. This will be worth it. Even Farthing might agree.'

CHAPTER FORTY-ONE

The bell rang as we entered the music shop and I gazed around, my mouth dropping open. Fiddles, yes, but other instruments too. The glow of brass caught the light from the window, dazzling me. Anything made of wood was buffed to a high shine the like of which I'd never seen, and a smell of varnish and wealth filled the shop.

'Take your pick, Covington, don't even glance at the price tags,' said Mr Darwin. 'You will try every fiddle in this shop, and I will buy the one that suits you best.'

The shopkeeper raised his eyebrows. He stood with his thumbs in his waistcoat pockets, and although his smile was friendly, he looked confused. I was freshly scrubbed and dressed in clean but well-worn sailor's cloth, white pants and blue tunic, and hatless. I now wore the other sailor's hand-me-downs, my own long since grown out of. I guessed I was not his usual customer.

My cheeks flushed and I gazed at the floor, wishing I had the weight of Farthing across my shoulders. Robbins was watching her for me, but she had whined when I'd climbed into the rowboat; we hadn't been separated since she came aboard. I should have stayed on deck. Fancy music shops weren't my world.

Mr Darwin took the shopkeeper aside, speaking close to his ear.

I clasped my hands together and watched the people walking past the window. Sydney was a new town, almost a city, and like none I'd seen on my travels. Echoes of England were everywhere, in the names of the parks and dusty roads, in the style of the houses. But all was fresh and bright under a crisp blue sky, nothing like the gloom and fog back home. Sydney was like a happier younger brother, still skipping in the street in knicker-bockers with a ball and hoop, while his older brother London hauled coal in the dark. As soon as I fetched Farthing, I'd be plenty pleased to explore at Mr Darwin's side and to take trips into the surrounding hills they called The Bush, although I had lost my enthusiasm for catching specimens.

The shopkeeper broke into a wide grin. 'Good day, Syms Covington!' he boomed, and gave my hand a hearty shake. 'The boy hisself. Your adventure, sonny, is the talk of the town, from harbour taverns to ladies' drawing rooms!'

I relaxed as I remembered this was Australia, not England, and that the rules of scruffy boys not being allowed in fancy shops didn't work quite the same here. Even the accent was different. The Australian voices sounded like everything was a question that hadn't been answered yet, as if anything could happen here, on the other side of the world.

I returned the shopkeeper's firm handshake with a squeeze. Arm slung across my shoulder, he led me along the row of fiddles, describing the benefits of different woods, pegs and strings, makers, dates and nationalities. I couldn't keep up.

Mr Darwin took a violin down from its hook.

'I know it can't replace Scratch. But I think it's time you coaxed out a tune again, don't you?'

I took the beautiful fiddle from my master. This instrument had a fancy chinrest and my jaw nestled perfectly. It felt different to the hard lines of Scratch. My hands shook.

When I drew the bow across the strings, I caught the scent of pine rosin and the first few notes took me back to the Narborough shore, filling the gaps in the tiny boat's seams with that precious rosin. By the second bar, I closed my eyes and I was spun back, way back, to when I was the smallest of boys, only just able to stretch my arm to grip the fiddle's neck, and Da's rough fingers covered my own as he helped me draw out my first note.

CHAPTER FORTY-TWO

The first two months back in England Mr Darwin and I were busy every long day making sure the specimens which had been shipped back were safely preserved and stored.

Now Mr Darwin hunched over his mahogany desk in his new rooms in Cambridge, working on a paper that would be his first presentation to The Geological Society in a few weeks' time.

I prised open another crate of specimens. This one was from Patagonia and was solely fossils. I lifted out a huge ancient bone and remembered the mother dragon attempting to heave herself from the lava. I shook my head, trying to scatter the memory. More of Mr Darwin's shipping arrived every day at Woolwich docks, and it seemed my job of cataloguing and then sending on to the appropriate gentlemen, would never be done. The day was cold and grey, as it had seemed to be every day since we had returned, and there'd be many more like it as it was only December. What I'd do for just a flash of that Australian sun on my face. But truly, I had little to complain about. Mr Darwin and I shared a comfortable lodging – my work was steady and well paid, and best of all, Farthing barely left my side.

I looked down at my hand, still pockmarked with scars from the burns, and suddenly I was back in the dragon's lair, then the lava was chasing me, Farthing racing ahead, the eggs clanking at my chest. My neck prickled with sweat, as I could feel that heat again. Too many memories today. I suddenly became aware Mr Darwin was calling me.

'Covington. Syms. *Covington*! You look like your body is in England, but your head somewhere else entirely.'

I had never quite gotten over the injury to my eardrum. I was now partly deaf in that ear, but I didn't like to remind Mr Darwin when he complained I wasn't listening. Especially as he had plenty of his own ailments to deal with. The young master was either strong and hearty, or laid low with chest palpitations and headaches. Nothing in between.

'Sorry sir—'

'No matter,' he said, tugging on his whiskers. 'Do you recall the small birds you preserved for your own collection, in the Galapagos?'

'The finches? I do. But your own specimens were the best examples.'

'Yes, yes,' he said, impatient, his eyes red-rimmed from long hours at his desk. 'But I labelled those myself and I'm afraid they are incomplete. Did you mark yours with the exact location and island?'

'Of course, sir. Just like you taught me,' I said.

'Well, thank the blazes you are a better student than I am a teacher. The ornithologist, Gould, from the Royal Society, has agreed to sketch and identify them for me, and my own records are sadly lacking.'

I opened a drawer in my bureau and found the logbook where I kept a neat record of my own small collection with dates, locations and sketches. I found the correct page and handed it to Mr Darwin. Seeing my drawings jogged my memory. The fumarole, the water . . .

'There's something else, sir. When I was on Narborough I observed a very similar bird, eating a yellow flower on a prickly pear. Its beak was longer and had more of a point to it than I'd seen before.'

My master looked up, there was an ink stain on his lip and his fluff of hair stood on end. 'Cactus flower? Can you remember well enough to sketch this bird for me, in detail?'

'Yes, I think so, sir,' I said.

'I'd like you to do that now then, Covington. Right away,' he said.

I took out a piece of drawing paper. Mr Darwin nodded and went back to his studies.

Farthing raised her head from the windowsill and gave a low hoot. She had been lazy lately, spending many hours laid out like this, as though soaking up the watery sun. Either that or by the fireplace. I wasn't sure England suited her, or me either after five years at sea. I ran my finger around the inside of my collar, starched and itchy.

Mr Darwin muttered. Farthing flicked up her head, then leapt to the floor and raced to the door. She scratched, hooting and growling.

'Covington, please. You know I can't have the lizard—'

A smart knock on the door. Without waiting for an answer, the housekeeper we shared with the other apartments, Mrs Harvey, stepped in. Her cheeks were pink and tendrils of pale hair escaped her cap. Farthing yelped and she jumped out of the way, and then the lizard flew out of the door. Mrs Harvey gasped and gave a small curtsey, her reddened hands clutching her apron.

'Farthing!' I called.

'Mr Darwin,' said Mrs Harvey, with forced calm, 'I simply cannot contend with more unexpected vermin. That ... newt thingummy ...' she waved in the direction Farthing had just ran, 'is bad enough. But I nearly killed this new little one with my broom.'

CHAPTER FORTY-THREE

Mr Darwin looked up from his work, frowning at Mrs Harvey, who was normally so steady and cheerful. She seemed awful out of sorts. What was this 'new little one' she was talking about?

'We have vermin? Please lay the poison, Mrs Harvey, and quickly,' snapped Mr Darwin. 'I cannot have pests about. We are working with delicate specimens.' He went back to his papers, frowning.

Mrs Harvey straightened her back and I saw by the tremor in her lips she was genuinely shocked. 'It's your *specimens* that are the problem, sir. The kitchen is simply not the place . . . such blazing eyes . . . mercy me, I thought it were a devil.'

I blinked at her. Little one? Blazing eyes? In the kitchen? Mr Darwin and I stood at the same time, scraping back our chairs, and I didn't wait for him. I raced down the narrow stairs.

The kitchen was warm and scented with fresh bread. Farthing had already reached the gap beside the stove and was standing on her hind legs, nose beneath the cloth that covered the open chest. The fabric was moving, and from inside came a rustling. My heart leapt into my throat and my hand shook as I went to remove the cloth, but I could not quite bring myself to do it.

Could this really be happening?

If all the eggs hatched there would be eight . . . eight *dragons*. I remembered their mother, her power and size.

Mr Darwin leant over me and lifted the cloth just enough to see. The bright eyes seemed too large for its wobbling head. The hatchling stopped shifting over its broken shell and stared directly up at us. I blinked and shook my head. I knew those eyes. I knew that intelligent, curious stare. It opened its mouth and the inside was pink, the edges rough, and I knew one day it would be rimmed with tiny teeth. It released a mewling sound like a cat begging for fish scraps. It was the size of a newborn kitten.

But it was far from a kitten. And not gold like its mother.

It was green. *Pistachio* green.

The hatchling wasn't a dragon. It was a . . . Farthing.

CHAPTER FORTY-FOUR

The hatchling couldn't be a . . . Farthing. Couldn't be. I'd seen the way the mother dragon had defended her brood, had tried to lift the egg in her mouth . . .

I pushed the cloth back entirely and leant forward to examine the newborn. To look for evidence on its tiny back, on its flanks. Like hatchling birds, the wings would be small, tiny, they would develop as the creature grew. The flanks were smoothly scaled, just as Farthing's were, and green.

No wings.

'Well, I wouldn't credit it if I had not seen it with my

own eyes. You are a wonder, Covington. A wonder!' exclaimed Mr Darwin. 'To have an egg survive that journey? The creature seems healthy and it is highly probable it is the same species as our Farthing. How singular for her to lead you to the nest when the eggs were in peril. Usually only the parent would show such protective behaviour.'

I didn't understand. I stared from Farthing to the hatchling and back again. Same shade of green. But Farthing was too small to be the mother . . . much too small. There had to be another explanation for this.

One of the eggs had *already hatched* in the dragon's lair.

'The shell, the shell that was in my foot,' I said, feeling gooseflesh rise along my arms.

Farthing leapt up on to the edge of the chest and poked her snout inside. The hatchling lifted its own tiny triangular face and sniffed. Farthing bumped its snout with her own. Before we could stop her, Farthing climbed into the makeshift nest and curled around the newborn. Like a cuckoo bird grown too large for the nest it stole.

'Well. I never saw the like,' said Mr Darwin softly.

The sliver of egg in my foot was from the egg that *Farthing* hatched from. My Farthing had somehow hatched earlier than the others.

Mr Darwin was right. They were the same species as Farthing, there was no doubt, and it made no sense.

Unless . . . they were *all* the dragon's young.

Farthing had survived the dragon fire.

The dragon did not attack Farthing in its lair.

Farthing had been desperate to save the eggs because inside them were her brothers or sisters.

As I thought it, I knew it was right.

Farthing was a dragon hatchling. The wedge shape of her head. The scales were green compared to her mother's gold, but somehow alike . . .

Mr Darwin and Mrs Harvey's voices were a distant buzz.

None of the other eggs moved.

'Farthing is from the same clutch,' I said.

I looked at Mr Darwin. His eyes were shining. History was being made here, without any mention of dragons.

An egg from the Galapagos, live and hatching was enough.

The truth was too much.

'Doesn't seem likely, but not impossible. We know nothing about the breeding of these reptiles, Farthing being quite unique,' he said.

'They are all . . . dragons,' I said.

'Dragons? Great heavens!' gasped Mrs Harvey. 'I will not have—'

'There's nothing to fear, Mrs Harvey,' said Mr Darwin, eyes flashing a warning to me beneath low brows, 'there is a species of reptile known as a Komodo Dragon. It is kept at the London Zoological Society. That is what Covington was referring to.'

I pinched my lips together. Could I be wrong?

Mr Darwin stood and smoothed the dust from his knees.

'I will contact the Zoological Society immediately. Covington, watch the hatchling, make sure it doesn't escape the chest. Mrs Harvey, I'm going to need you to find a temporary cage for our new guest. Here—' He wrote something on the notepad he kept in his pocket and handed it to her.

He fell silent.

'Looks to me like the poor little demon needs feeding,' said Mrs Harvey.

'They eat fish,' I blurted.

'I'll mix a pap from bread crusts and milk,' said Mrs Harvey, ignoring me as she usually did. 'You'll need to feed them from a spoon. As a girl, I raised a fallen chick from a nest—'

Darwin interrupted her. 'Mrs Harvey. Please make haste before we have lizards overrunning the apartments.'

'Well,' she huffed, as she pulled off her apron and smoothed her hair back under her cap. 'If you are going to feed them the mackerel I'd planned for supper, then it will be cold cuts again this evening.'

'If you could just leave the mackerel out, thank you, Mrs Harvey.'

'You'll choke them to death if you feed it to them whole. It will need cutting and mashing, no bones—'

'Please do not bother yourself, Mrs Harvey. Covington here is rather an expert on these . . . lizards.'

CHAPTER FORTY-FIVE

The eggs hatched one by one, over the course of the following month. Farthing slept with them, curled in a mass of green scales inside the chest, and just before each egg hatched she would fetch me from the study. I fed them with mashed mackerel on a tiny spice spoon.

There was at least two days between each hatching; a couple of the eggs took three. This was something Mr Darwin had never witnessed before. He now thought it possible that I was right, about Farthing being a sibling to these newborns, maybe even from the same clutch. His colleagues visited and were also surprised. Clutches of eggs always hatched in one go. Well, not these eggs.

Not so surprising to me. After all, no one had ever come across a clutch of dragon eggs before.

But on that point, I kept my mouth shut.

My room had become the lizard nursery, while a special enclosure was being built for them at the Zoological Society. They slept and ate a lot. And they grew. They grew quickly. The first to hatch was now almost the size of Farthing.

But one egg was left in the chest by the stove. One. And it had been five days since the last hatched.

'Mr Darwin, Covington, it's started!' called Mrs Harvey from the kitchen. By now she'd taken quite a shine to the 'giant newts'.

We looked up from our desks at the same time.

'Take a note to Mrs Whitby please, Mrs Harvey,' said Mr Darwin. 'I saw her only last night at the British Association presentation, and she is staying nearby. She was so desperate to witness a hatching.'

Mrs Mary Anne Whitby was one of Mr Darwin's regular correspondents and an experimenter in silkworm breeding. She arrived in a cloud of violet-scented grey skirts and a sensible black bonnet, and spoke with the master in quiet yet enthusiastic tones. The last egg was vibrating and shivering. Farthing peered over at it but rested her snout against the rim of the chest and did not move. The movement and tapping of the egg slowed.

Mr Darwin had already directed me not to interfere with any of the hatchings.

Farthing whined.

'Go on then, Farthing. Give it a nudge or something?' I whispered. Farthing twitched her head to one side but did not move.

'There's a runt in every litter, and it will soon die,' said Mrs Whitby, a monocle clamped to her eye, 'and good fortune for you, Mr Darwin – a specimen to dissect. Sooner rather than later mind, as it will quickly spoil.'

Mr Darwin rubbed two fingers against his forehead. 'It is true that the young creature inside may not be fit enough to survive, and that has a strong reason in nature …'

I pictured Mr Darwin in sleeve protectors, his scalpels and tools lined up in front of him. I'd seen it often enough, a thing that had been living, reduced to a carcass, pinned and labelled, then a series of sketches and observations, and finally just mess for me to clear.

The master caught me staring at him, stopped talking and swallowed.

The last dragon egg gave a sorry little shiver.

CHAPTER FORTY-SIX

I shifted so I was positioned between Mrs Whitby and the treasure-chest nest. What to do? I looked at Farthing and remembered back on Narborough, when she'd followed, hiding from me. I had played Scratch and she'd listened.

'Please, a bit more time,' I said.

'No rush, Covington,' said Mr Darwin.

I darted into the other room to collect my new fiddle. Settled by the stove, I played a rum jig, one that had never failed to rouse the sleepiest of old seamen into activity on ship.

Mr Darwin gave me an encouraging nod.

'These creatures are incredibly important to Science, they may be the only ones left of their kind if the volcano engulfed the island. It could be that the vibrations of the violin assist with the hatching, and a living specimen is far more valuable,' he said.

Mrs Whitby gave a delicate snort, but didn't argue.

I thought on what Mr Darwin had said. When I played, the lowest notes produced the most detectable vibration, right in the centre of my chest. I buttoned up my open waistcoat almost to the top and then lifted the last egg from the nest and rested it, tucked into the open buttons, against my heart. Its warmth passed through my shirt and vest. I lifted my fiddle and played a slow ballad.

When I finished the tune, the egg continued to vibrate between my ribs. The hatchling inside was still alive, and I was sure it could hear and feel me.

'Your husband mentioned you were a fine alto in your church choir, Mrs Whitby?' said Darwin.

A hymn. That was it.

I played 'Amazing Grace' again and the lady dropped in, her voice clear and steady. The melody did not echo like it had in the lava tube of the Galapagos, but it took me back there.

I looked down without halting the tune. A fine crack in the surface of the egg. I stopped playing and held the egg, which filled my cupped hands.

Ignoring Mrs Whitby's muttering, I did not ask Mr Darwin's permission before I gently eased apart the crack. The lizard inside reached out a tiny claw and then the egg split in two across my palms and I was holding another miniature Farthing, perfect, smaller than the others, her eyes unfocused but bright.

The tiny beast gazed at me, head wobbling on her spindly neck. She strained up, then lost her balance and tumbled backwards into her broken shell.

This little one had a streak of silver shot through one of her copper eyes, shiny as a sixpence.

CHAPTER FORTY-SEVEN

'Welcome to the world, little Sixpence,' I whispered. Farthing leapt on to the side of the chest and curled around the youngest of her siblings, as she had done with each newborn. There was a hesitation in her jump, a lack of energy that made my stomach churn. Farthing wasn't herself lately, slower. Quieter. The wound on her side still hadn't fully healed. In the last month the green of her scales had changed, they had a sheen almost like mother of pearl. I didn't think even Werner had a name for that colour.

Sixpence nibbled mashed fish from the spice spoon. I waited for Mrs Whitby to leave and for Mr Darwin to come back to the kitchen.

In between waiting, and making sure the eggs safely hatched, I had been researching, thinking and watching Farthing; the way, when she greeted me, her ruff was now slow to rise. She blinked more slowly. She seemed flatter somehow. But how to make Mr Darwin understand that these animals didn't belong here?

Because London was really not the place for dragons.

'Sir, may I discuss . . . an important matter with you?' I said, tripping over words more formal than I was used to.

'Of course. Here,' he said, passing me a small brandy, 'to toast the safe birth of another little miracle.'

I took a sip and grimaced.

'You see, sir; it was the wings that put me off when I was on Narborough. Plus the fact that the mother dragon was intent on removing me, then burning me, so I didn't get much chance to really look at her.' I was rambling – I tried to slow down. 'But a lot of things make sense. The dragon had the same type of scales, the same shaped body and face as these creatures. And their eyes. Farthing's are copper and the dragon's are gold, but they are both – extraordinary, in the same way. As for the difference in size and colour, differences like that between a mother and its young aren't unknown in the animal kingdom. Are they? Sir?'

My words tripped each other up, I needed to make him see what was so obvious to me now. He took a large gulp of his brandy and was silent.

'. . . it's like when a caterpillar turns into a butterfly. Or when a tadpole turns into a frog!' A deep crease had now formed between Mr Darwin's eyes, but I had to finish. 'The dragon is a species that hatches without wings, they must develop later, sir, maybe only when they are fully grown. And at some point their colour will change from green to gold. Look.' I pointed to Farthing's scales, but the sun must have disappeared behind a cloud because even I couldn't see the shining glint any more.

Mr Darwin peered at Farthing and shook his head very slightly.

'You are suggesting these lizards will undergo a . . . metamorphosis? And become dragons?'

'Yes! Why not?' I said, my heart leaping in my chest.

'Because aside from everything else, they are reptiles, Covington. Reptiles do not undergo metamorphosis.'

'And mammals don't fly, but look at bats!' I was speaking rudely, but it couldn't be helped.

Mr Darwin sighed and rubbed his temples.

'This must bring back a lot of memories for you, my dear fellow,' he sipped his brandy and lowered his voice, 'but you have to understand, this is a critical time for me. Critical. The ideas I am working on are important, and incredibly . . . sensitive. I must build my reputation before they can be credited. I cannot afford any controversy.'

'But, it's the truth. I know you see it, sir,' I burst out.

'Covington. The only miracle I see here is a boy who saved my life,' his voice dropped even further, 'a boy brave beyond reason who brought back a scientific marvel.'

I looked down at Sixpence. She seemed smaller than the others had been. Next to her dark slick scales, Farthing looked tired and dusty. Farthing was just a baby herself. The eggs had all survived, yet I felt a creeping dread. Mr Darwin cleared his throat and stood, straightening his pocket watch.

'Now, we can't keep a room full of growing reptiles, the skirting boards are already in tatters. Their enclosure at the London Zoological Society is ready, and as soon as this little one is strong enough, they will all be homed there. They will be safe, the environment health giving, with more room for their natural behavioural patterns to develop and be studied.'

Mr Darwin's tone was brisk. He'd talked to me about this, but I wasn't ready. I opened my mouth to protest, then looked at Farthing and closed it again. She couldn't stay here, it was making her unwell. The thought of being away from her . . . but I couldn't be selfish and try to keep her by my side, this new enclosure might help her.

I had no choice but to trust Mr Darwin, even if he didn't trust me.

CHAPTER FORTY-EIGHT

The carriage trundled over the cobbles and Mr Darwin took his customary place by the window, likely hoping for breeze but instead inhaling the heavy summer stink of London. I offered him some smelling salts, but he declined with downturned lips and a shake of his head, taking a snort of snuff instead, which resulted in three quick sneezes. As always, he was a poor traveller, not as ill as he was when he was at sea, but he suffered nonetheless. I sighed. Farthing and her family had been rehomed at the London Zoological Society for eight months now and I wondered when I would stop missing her. Our weekly visit to see them made my insides churn – my heart leaping with excitement, my stomach curling in dread. The lizards had been officially named Galapagos green lizards, but soon became known as Darwin's Dragons. The Komodo dragons were in the enclosure next to them in the reptile house at the London Zoological Society and their joint space became known as Dragon Corner.

Darwin's *Dragons*. And in my mind, I always thought of them as dragons. I was the only keeper of their secret identity. There was nobody I could even try to convince. If Mr Darwin wouldn't believe me, then no one else would either.

Mr Darwin's talk for the Royal Society had been very well received. He'd outlined his geological findings from the voyage, describing the singular animals of the Galapagos in great detail, and displayed our preserved specimens in their jars and glass cases. We moved to London in May, my master making me his secretary, with both room and board and an excellent wage for a boy of my age.

On the outside, fortune had smiled upon a simple fiddler's son, an orphan who had run off to sea. From the lowest rank on board, I had risen to be manservant and now the secretary of a most distinguished gentleman, making a name for himself in the world of Science.

Yet I could not sleep at night, and spent my days in

what Scratch would have called 'a maudlin'. I made mistakes in my work, and my belly knotted up like ship's rigging.

The dragons' home, the London Zoological Society, was the largest collection of wildlife in the world. Farthing and the others grew up playful and competitive, fighting but never injuring each other. They slept as they had when they were newly hatched, balled up together. Except Farthing, who always lay separately, facing them, watchful. She remained protective of them even when they caught up with her in size. They were unlike any other reptile the zoological society had encountered, curious about the other inhabitants, sociable and with an impressive array of calls that delighted visiting society members – the only persons admitted into the zoological park grounds.

Their hoots even attracted the attention of passers-by outside the walls, who lingered at Dragon Corner to listen to their calls so often a stand was set up selling hot 'dragon' pies.

The lizards responded to their keepers and answered to their names. Early studies suggested they were nearly as intelligent as the apes, and of much higher intelligence than their supposed cousins, the Komodo dragons.

The coach pulled up and we were quickly admitted

through the gates, the pair of us familiar to the guards.

We passed the barred dome of the raven cage, flicks of the bright wings of macaws inside. Mr Darwin took an unfamiliar turn through the rows of enclosures.

I stopped.

'Come, Covington. The society has recently procured a new . . .'

The word 'inmate' sprang into my mind.

'. . . guest. I know you are impatient to get to Farthing, but please indulge me.'

He led me to a low building and rapped on the door. It was opened by a keeper.

'Her name is Jenny,' said Mr Darwin, 'and we have seen nothing like her. She is an orangutan from the jungles of Borneo, and quite remarkable.'

CHAPTER FORTY-NINE

I followed Mr Darwin inside the small building. Along one wall was a barred area with a stone floor, scattered with hay. Jenny the orangutan was the size of a child of around four years old, had been clothed in a flowered dress, and had wispy reddish hair covering her long limbs. She lumbered over to the bars, knuckles almost reaching the floor, and gripped the metal with strong leathery fingers. Her heavy brow rose, a peak of red fluff stuck up from the top of her head, and beneath it her eyes shone, dark brown – sharp, but soft at the same time. I was taken aback by the strange little creature, so like a person, yet so different. I wondered if she had willingly worn the dress, as she clearly had no need for it. When I smiled at her, Jenny bared her large teeth with a clicking sound, and then turned away.

'She doesn't like it when you show your teeth,' said the keeper. 'Jenny. This is Mr Darwin, come to visit you.' He fastened the door to the building behind us, then unlocked the door to her caged area and passed Mr Darwin a green apple. My master stepped inside the cage and surprised me by sitting down on the floor. He held out the apple on the palm of his hand like he might be feeding a horse. Jenny came over to him, sniffed at the apple but did not take it.

'She has recently been fed, sir,' said the keeper.

Jenny turned back to the bars where I was waiting, fascinated. I took the handkerchief from my pocket and held it out to her, raising my eyes at the keeper who nodded his permission.

The little orangutan snatched the handkerchief and sniffed it, without taking her sharp gaze from me. I chuckled, but kept my lips closed this time, and she pouted her lips in response then rested the handkerchief on her head, looking up at it. I looked up at my own cap, then took it off. Jenny took the handkerchief off her head.

Mr Darwin got to his feet. 'Well done, Covington. You see how she mimics; her behaviour is quite childlike.

I intend to study her as she becomes more used to me. But that's enough for today,' he said.

The master's voice was alive with passion, the same passion I'd seen when the first dragon egg hatched. The little ape capered around her cage, throwing my handkerchief in the air and watching as it fell, then picking it up again, over and over. She was so far from her jungle home, from others of her kind. I remembered how that felt and gripped the cold bars.

'You can keep the handkerchief, Jenny,' I said.

CHAPTER FIFTY

I approached Farthing's enclosure in the same way as always, counting the dragons. Farthing was already at the bars and raced to my side. I crouched to greet her, and she nudged my hand until I scratched her cheek. Her ruff rose, but the scales didn't quite align, and her eyes seemed dusty, dim. I counted the rest of the dragons, nine including Farthing – there was Sixpence, Quartz, Basalt, Granite, Magma, Slate, Obsidian and Marble. Mr Darwin had named them after rocks of the earth where they had been found.

Farthing snorted hot air into my palm as I waded to the back of the lizard enclosure in my heavy fisherman's gaiters. Mr Darwin spoke with the head keeper, taking notes. One of the dragons lay listlessly beneath a brazier of hot coals, mud covering his green scales.

'Quartz was like that all day yesterday, and hasn't stirred today, sir,' called out the keeper.

I slopped over to Quartz, through the mud, and laid a hand beneath his chin. He snorted but didn't open his eyes, not a slice of copper to be seen, even when I whistled. The smaller of his claws was white and shiny, so we had called him after the crystal. I stroked this claw now.

'Stay bricky, boy,' I said quietly.

'Mr Darwin,' I called. The young gentleman waded halfway over to me, looked down at Quartz, and nodded.

'Keep a close eye on this one,' said Mr Darwin to the keeper.

I shook my head. I didn't see how a close eye could help.

Mr Darwin stood beside me, pulling at his long side whiskers thoughtfully. 'Interesting that Quartz seems weaker than the rest, yet he is one of the largest, and has been stronger in general. It would appear that some individuals are simply more adaptable to a change in conditions.'

Despair dropped through my chest like a lead weight as Mr Darwin walked away, scribbling in his notebook.

It would never be warm enough. We could never recreate the lava plains of the Galapagos, the tunnels, the dry heat. Not here. I had brought these animals to a damp murky city, out of the centre of a volcano.

'And the others – how is their weight?' I asked the keeper.

'No change,' he said.

'Well, they are fully grown now, so that's expected,' replied Mr Darwin.

I had nothing to say. Not in front of the keeper. The dragons were now the size of labrador dogs, but they were far from fully grown. They were growing larger, but not heavier because their muscles were weakening. No one understood – the dragons were still babies.

'How has Farthing been?' I said, afraid of the answer.

'Oh, she's still herself most of the time, bossing around the others,' the keeper smiled and nodded over my shoulder. Farthing reared up on her hind legs and hooted. I threw her a half-rotten sardine, and instead of catching it, she twisted and flicked it with her tail straight into the mouth of Magma, one of her sisters. I laughed.

No reptile expert had been able to confirm the dragon's genders, but Mr Darwin and I had agreed that we thought the females had slightly narrower snouts than the males.

We had made modifications over the last two months to improve their living area, giving them live fish to catch in a small pond, and rocks where they could take shelter, plus the braziers had just been installed in case they suffered from the lack of heat. But the ground was always muddy, as the enclosure was on soil not rock, the stagnant water could not be kept fresh, and no matter how many keepers were employed to clean out, there was a rancid stench.

'Still up to her tricks then?' I said, throwing Farthing another fish. At least she had her appetite. For now.

'Sometimes, sir,' the keeper lowered his voice, side-glanced at Mr Darwin and leant closer towards me. 'Your visits raise her spirits. Then after, she always paces the bars longer than the others.'

My face must have clearly painted my feelings at hearing this.

'Sorry, lad, but you did say you wanted to know everything,' he whispered.

I nodded, cleared my throat. 'Yes.'

I felt a sudden burst of anger. I waded over to Mr Darwin on the edge of the enclosure.

'Sir, we have to do something. You saw Quartz. They aren't doing well here, they are ill—'

Mr Darwin's bushy brows drew together.

'They are simply reaching maturity, Covington. Fully

grown, you can expect them to be less playful, they may be slower during cooler weather—'

'They are *not* fully grown,' I interrupted in a hissing voice, flushing at my boldness, but not able to stop now, 'they are all babies, you know they are . . . and they are ill! They will grow to the size of a . . . a . . . whale!'

Mr Darwin's eyes flashed. He glanced around at the keepers who had stepped away and were politely getting on with cleaning a corner of the enclosure, pretending not to listen.

'Covington, I thought I had very clearly explained the consequences of this manner of talk,' said Mr Darwin, 'my reputation is at the most delicate stage—'

'It is the truth, sir. You have to help them,' I said, meeting his eyes, pleading, dismayed to feel a sob in the back of my throat. 'We have to send them . . . back.'

'Back? You don't know what you are asking—'

'Mr Darwin, sir,' a park warden in black uniform interrupted.

'What is it, man?' snapped Mr Darwin. I had never heard him speak like that to a stranger before.

'I am afraid you must leave,' said the warden.

'Impossible. We have only just arrived, and have important scientific work—'

'Nothing I can do, sir, the park must be empty for this particular guest—'

'Thank you, Chatham, that will do. These are no ordinary visitors,' interrupted a new voice, clear and high as a bell, and with a clipped upper class accent I'd rarely heard the like of.

I turned at the same time as Mr Darwin. Outside the enclosure stood a woman dressed in an apple-green silk gown, sparkling with fancy embroidery. She tipped back her lace parasol to reveal a serious girlish face, framed with glossy brown ringlets. A retinue of guards and companions gathered behind her.

'Your Majesty,' Darwin stuttered, bowing deeply.

It was Victoria, the Queen of England.

CHAPTER FIFTY-ONE

'Your Majesty,' I repeated, and bowed too, painfully aware of my muddy gaiters, peasant's neckerchief and rough waistcoat. I was dressed for an animal enclosure, not a royal visit. Mr Darwin had mentioned that the new queen herself had taken an interest in the dragons, but I hadn't dreamt we would see her here. The coronation had only been little more than a year ago and she looked younger in person than I had expected. Our queen was yet to turn twenty, closer to my age than to Mr Darwin's.

'You are Mr Darwin's servant, the boy who found my remarkable dragons in their eggs?' she said.

'Yes, ma'am,' I managed, bowing again, but thinking of the word 'my'. She was staking her claim.

'Well, come forward, no need for ceremony. I am sure I was the last person you were expecting to see. What is your name again? I will speak with you and your master, both.'

Myself and Mr Darwin stepped forward at the same time, and I forced myself to meet her grey gaze.

'My name is Syms Covington, ma'am,' I said, hardly able to believe I was talking to the Queen.

'Of course it is, I remember Mr Darwin spoke quite at length of your bravery at my Royal Society luncheon. I would like to read your own account of events on Narborough Island some time – I do so adore a tale of survival against the odds. Almost as much as I enjoy the sight of exotic and intriguing animals. Like my dragons here.' She frowned, and shook her finger at my master as if he were a naughty child. 'Their health deteriorates. This is unacceptable, as I have become most fond of them. What is your answer to this, Mr Darwin?'

The young queen's eyes were wide and expectant, used to receiving the answer she wanted, when she wanted it.

'We have improved their diet and provided more shelter, to make the area more similar to the natural—'

'I know what *has* been done, but it has clearly not been effective,' said the Queen, dismissing him with a wave of the hand. 'Look at them. They are quiet, listless, off their food. Now, I would like to know what is *going* to be done, before we lose one of these dear creatures.'

Mr Darwin cleared his throat and although I did not look at him, I knew his face would be reddening.

Mr Darwin might not be willing to help me, but maybe the Queen of England would.

'Your Majesty,' I said, barely able to believe I was speaking in Mr Darwin's place, and directly to the Queen, 'the lizards must be returned to their home. Some animals don't do well in captivity and they are the last of their kind. Ma'am.'

I bowed. When I rose, I saw Mr Darwin's cheeks were red and his lips a thin line. I avoided his eyes.

'Returned to their home? The ... Galapagos Islands?' said the Queen, her eyebrows arching.

This was it. While Farthing and the others were still strong enough to make the voyage, the Queen would make it happen. They could be released on the biggest island, Albemarle, into the lava tubes ...

'Impossible!' her laugh tinkled high, but to me it sounded like a funeral bell.

'Covington. You found them, you witnessed them in their environs. They are cave dwellers, are they not?'

'Yes, ma'am, they seem to be, although there were far from scientific observations—'

She waved her hand again, cutting me off. 'Of course they were not scientific. You were a terrified young boy, left alone, marooned amidst a volcanic eruption!'

Behind, her retinue laughed with her. I supposed I should be flattered the Queen knew of me, but I felt like I was their entertainment.

The Queen leant in closer, her eyes suddenly shrewd. She tapped my arm once with her small white-gloved hand, and lowered her voice.

'I have decided I will make my interest in Darwin's Dragons official. These animals will be protected under a royal charter, meaning they belong to the monarchy.' She didn't stop, so I didn't have time to figure out what this would mean for Farthing and the others. 'I will discuss my plans only with you, Covington, and Mr Darwin,' she added as an afterthought, 'as you know the animals best. I will send a carriage at nine p.m. one week from today.'

With a curt nod, barely acknowledging our deep bows, Queen Victoria disappeared beneath her lace parasol and walked at a clipped pace back to her retinue.

Mr Darwin's eyebrows had disappeared beneath the rim of his top hat. He lowered his voice as we made our way back to the carriage.

'You will not undermine me in that way again, Covington. Do you understand?' he said, his voice quiet but not at all soft.

I swallowed and dropped my chin. 'I am sorry, sir.'

The silence felt heavy and desperate between us.

'Where do you think the carriage she sends will take us?' I asked.

'I have no idea, Covington. But we will find out soon enough.'

CHAPTER FIFTY-TWO

On the day following our visit to the Zoological Society and the bizarre meeting with the Queen, Mr Darwin and I worked in his study, silent. For once, it did not feel like the calm quiet of two people long used to being holed up with just each other for company. Mr Darwin did not look up at me at all, and tugged his whiskers more than usual. I wanted to beg him again, to do anything he could to get the dragons back to the Galapagos. With his naval connections, with his standing in the Royal Society, my young master was becoming an important man. But I'd asked him already, the answer had been clear, and I'd been chided for my insolence. It was past four when I received the message from the keepers at the Zoological Park that we were needed immediately. They didn't say why.

'It's Quartz,' I said.

Mr Darwin gathered his hat and cane.

'You don't know that, dear boy,' he said softly. I hoped he was right.

He was not.

I felt it in the soupy afternoon fog, I heard it in the roll of the carriage wheels, I saw it in the grim face of the warden as he opened the gates.

We detected the dragon calls as we passed the other quiet enclosures, a whining sound, high and tragic.

I quickened my step.

The keeper's eyes were red rimmed. 'We don't know what to do with them; we can't get them away from Quartz. We thought we should send for you, before we . . . Farthing has simply been pacing the bars. I've never seen them show any sign of aggression before this but now – she . . . she's warning us off.'

I nodded and stepped into the enclosure.

'Covington, I think . . .'

Mr Darwin trailed off. I would never be afraid of Farthing.

The dragons were mounded around Quartz, bundled together like when they slept, in a tangled ball. They were keening – a high-pitched drawn-out whine, a sound to put your teeth on edge, to twang the strings of your heart. Farthing was the only one who stood outside of the group. Mr Darwin was by my side, but when Farthing flicked around and snarled at him, he stumbled back against the bars.

'My word,' he said.

'I'll go in on my own, sir.'

He nodded.

I approached Farthing. She growled and darted at me, grabbing my shirt sleeve and jerking hard. The thin cotton ripped off in her mouth. I stood my ground and her growl turned into a mournful drone. I was taken back to the lava tunnel, when she'd led me to rescue the eggs as the volcano erupted. She wanted me to follow her now.

I approached the dragons, who were nudging Quartz with their snouts. At his head, fish had been laid out on the mud, all untouched. Sixpence picked up a fish in her jaws and gently nudged it at her brother. Quartz's head slipped off his front claw on to the mud.

You'd think a sleeping creature and a dead creature would be very similar, but there was every difference. A light had gone out. My heart was a lead weight, plummeting.

Quartz was already gone, but it didn't stop me shuffling forward on to my knees in the mud, to hold my hand against his snout, praying for his hot breath to warm my palm.

My hand became colder. I was cold all over. I swallowed back the urge to vomit.

I removed my hand and bowed my head, as tears seeped from my tight-closed eyes. Farthing growled so loud, my deaf ear rang. She picked up my hand softly, but firmly, in her jaw and laid it back on Quartz's head.

Farthing manoeuvred so her snout almost met mine, her copper eyes blinking, ruff of scales flattened back. She growled again, trailing into a whimper, and the others joined in with a cacophony of whines, and mournful howls. Quartz's lifeless body trembled with their nudges and his one white claw sunk out of sight, into the London mud.

When I took my hand from his head again, Farthing snarled and tried to snatch it up. She didn't understand.

I'd saved the eggs from the volcano; I'd saved them all. She believed I could save Quartz now.

I placed my hands either side of her wedge-shaped face as she whined and pawed the ground.

'You know I would if I could,' I whispered.

CHAPTER FIFTY-THREE

With Mr Darwin's guiding hand on my shoulder, I was eventually persuaded to leave the dragon enclosure. The dragons continued to mourn Quartz for a full day, and then took turns to guard his body for another. Finally, Quartz's body could be removed, and the enclosure was quiet. The dragons continued their normal routine, the two who had become listless remained listless. The others sometimes played with each other, and caught fish. But Farthing now paced the bars for hours at a time. She did not return to how she was before. I was able to visit more often as Mr Darwin was studying Jenny the orangutan, but my being there didn't calm Farthing. She tugged at my sleeve, she whined, growled, hooted. She still believed I could *do* something.

Mr Darwin and I spent our days in silence, him absorbed with his new notes on ape behaviour. I could not even be cheered by the violin. I had to find a way to rescue Farthing and the others. Quartz was gone. Who would be next?

I couldn't even think it might be Farthing, my heart wouldn't let me. But they were in London Zoological Park, guarded night and day. And even if I could – no. It was impossible, and I felt sick to my bones.

I couldn't even take some time with my maudlin. Mr Darwin and I had an appointment with the Queen.

A black carriage drew up outside our lodgings just before nine p.m., as arranged. A grim sort of fellow, older than both of us put together and sporting an outmoded bushy grey moustache, ushered us in to the plain but rich interior without a word. The carriage had thick velvet curtains, so it felt like being inside a black box. It was lit inside by a swinging oil lamp, and I flashed back to the buccaneer in the cave. How many nights had he spent in utter darkness, beneath the boat, alone? I thought I'd rather be there than here, watching the dragons die, slowly, with nothing I could do.

Neither Darwin nor I spoke, he seemed as lost in thought as I was. Our destination had something to do with the dragons, that was all we knew. The idea of Farthing and the others under the Queen's protection gave me the jitters. It was probably some form of treason to even think that I did not totally trust the young queen, but it was the truth.

The carriage was heading out of the city. After a silent journey of around twenty minutes, the road beneath the carriage became rougher and we gripped the handrails. Mr Darwin's eyes widened in alarm and I gave him the smallest of smiles. For once, I was not prepared for his motion sickness, and did not fancy giving him my tweed cap for the purpose. The carriage soon drew to a halt, and our driver opened the door and ushered us out. We were on a bare stretch of land, the moon lighting a low building and what looked like a tower, similar to those found at a mine. There was also another carriage, much larger than ours and with a trailer attached behind, on which rested a large crate, plain black.

'What is our location, sir?' said Mr Darwin to the driver.

'I have my orders, mister. You are requested to enter the mine. I am instructed to tell you it is perfectly safe, but to say no more. If you do not wish to enter the choice is yours and I am to return you forthwith, sir,' said the guard.

Mr Darwin and I looked at each other, although there was no question. I was heading underground for the first time since I had rescued the eggs.

We swung the oil lamps as we followed another silent man through the wide underground tunnel. My heart thumped and sweat beaded cool on my forehead as I recalled the last time I had been underground, racing against the boiling lapping tongue of lava; I still sported the scars to my legs.

The tunnel was not far from the surface with walls of damp pale chalk. It was wide and reached high, like the lava tubes, but it was much more cool and dank. Water dripped from the ceiling, and I wondered if Mr Darwin might know where we were, because there could not be so many disused mine workings such a short distance from London. The man led us through winding tunnels, all large and high, until noises could be heard. The echoes grew louder, and I recognized a female voice and something else.

A hoot! The dragons. How? It didn't matter. Not a growl, not a whine, but a joyful hoot, and a splash of water. I had not heard the dragons make such a sound in so long, I grinned and began to run, overtaking the man leading us, following the hoots and splashes. Around the next corner, I stopped in amazement. A wave of heat hit my face. Large braziers in wrought iron cages lit the area, like small bonfires lining the walls, red-hot coals illuminating a huge hollow in the centre. Iron bars and a gate covered the entrance, and inside was a giant pool, ten times the size of the muddy puddle at the Zoological Society, and surrounded by rocks. Only three of the dragons were there, one swimming, head above water, one rolling in the shallows and a third curled beneath a brazier of red coals.

'On my word—' exclaimed Mr Darwin.

'It's, it's . . .' I stumbled over my words. The red coals, the rocks, the darkness. It was the closest thing I'd seen to the Galapagos caves.

CHAPTER FIFTY-FOUR

A small neat figure stepped out of the shadows. This time Queen Victoria wore stout boots, a long black cape and a large old-fashioned bonnet, that shadowed and sharpened her features. Two uniformed men and an older lady stood behind her. Her Majesty broke into a controlled smile.

Mr Darwin and I immediately removed our hats, bowing low before our queen. How could she be *here*? She was the Queen. And I supposed that was why she was here; she could be exactly where she liked.

'You are pleased with my dragons' new lodgings?' she said, her clipped voice echoing around the caves.

'Your Majesty, I—'

She gave Mr Darwin a dismissive wave and stepped towards me, head cocked to one side.

'Mr Covington, I was most perplexed to hear the news about poor dear Quartz. A beautiful animal. Please tell me – and you must be honest now – is this of any approximation to the environment the lizards experienced on their native Narborough Island?'

I clutched the rim of my cap so hard it crumpled. The Queen of England wanted my opinion. The cave was still damp, the rocks were not volcanic, they could not roam . . . but compared to the enclosure at the Zoological Society . . .

I replied, 'Yes, ma'am. Yes, it is.'

A flame of hope bloomed in my chest. I wanted to trust her. I needed someone to help me save them.

'Ma'am, can I ask where Farthing is?'

The Queen explained that she had only transported three to start with, to trial the new environment. Farthing had refused to leave the others. She smiled, and then questioned me again, about the temperature, the darkness of the cave in which the lizard eggs had been found, and about the behaviour I had witnessed from Farthing on the island. Mr Darwin stayed silent. All the while I could barely resist watching the animals. I recognized Sixpence, Magma and Basalt. Sixpence played in the water, and Magma and Basalt inspected the braziers. They had not been so animated in over a year, and I told Her Majesty so.

She clapped her hands in delight.

'I see you are keen to greet them,' she said, and removed a key from a pouch at her belt. 'Only I and a guard will have a copy of this key, but Mr Darwin may keep a key to the mine entrance,' she said. I felt a blast of chill, even as the heat inside the cave rose. This was a private secret place, under the Queen's full control, unlike the Zoological Park, which was in the public eye.

I waded around the outside of the pool, with no care for my boots or trousers. I knelt before Sixpence under the brazier, and the heat tickled my cheeks.

The dragon opened her eyes, and there was no sign of the dull film that I had seen at the zoological park. I held out my hand and Sixpence butted it gently.

The Queen was behind me. Bonnet removed, sturdy boots and gaiters beneath her long skirts, tucked high above the water. I could not believe I was wading in a cave pool with the English monarch.

She passed me a sardine, and I threw it for Sixpence. I thought of the young dragon's magnificent mother, swooping golden through the Galapagos skies.

These animals were not made for cheap circus tricks.

'So, you see they are already better,' said Queen

Victoria. She whistled and Basalt, the largest male, swam towards the Queen, rolling on his belly and then surfacing next to her with a chirp. He sat back on his haunches and she held out a scrap of fish. She whistled again and he nodded towards the fish, but she withheld it.

Then Basalt whined back to her in the same tone.

The Queen's laugh rang high through the cave, echoing, and Basalt raised his ruff, and hooted.

Could now be the time to tell Her Majesty the truth about what they were? She cared for the dragons. If I told her, she could help them. Even if this place made them well again, there would be a new problem. They would grow, and grow.

I remembered the mother dragon spouting fire.

'I taught him that, Covington,' said the Queen, 'he only learnt it when I found out he adores a smoked sardine, the naughty brute. Of course, these beasts are no patch on my dogs. They may be as intelligent, yet not nearly so amenable, even to their queen and protector,' she said.

And with that, I knew I could not tell her. She saw them as brutes and beasts, and I had no evidence, nothing to prove what they truly were. They did these tricks to please us, not themselves. This cave was still a prison, the Queen's prison, but a prison nonetheless. The Queen was *annoyed* by Quartz's death. Annoyed was not how I felt, or how Farthing and the others felt, it was not the same as heartbroken.

I looked sideways at the Queen's young face, a cheek as smooth and pale as marble. Her small soft hands in their dark gloves, a girl tended by an army of maids since birth. What was she doing *here*?

I thought I understood. As a child, she had barely left the palace, she was known to have been kept closeted at Kensington and to have been so enraged by her strict upbringing she sent her own mother away after her coronation. Now she was Queen and could go where she liked. What would I do, if I were her?

I would do exactly what took my fancy. And these exotic animals took her fancy, nothing more.

'I have arranged to have the rest of the dragons relocated here tonight. Only I, members of my retinue and you and Mr Darwin will be permitted to enter until they are fully themselves again.'

I wished I could have some of her confidence.

Mr Darwin stepped forward. 'Your Majesty. The Zoological Society—'

'The Zoological Society were keeping these animals in great discomfort, a veritable mire of mud and stink, and one has already died,' she said, chin raised. 'Are they of more value to Science alive or dead, Mr Darwin?'

PART SIX

*There is no fundamental difference between man
and animals in their ability to feel pleasure
and pain, happiness, and misery.*

CHARLES DARWIN, *THE DESCENT OF MAN*

CHAPTER FIFTY-FIVE

It was a note from the London Zoological Society that drove me to search out the storm drain leading to the river.

When Mr Darwin opened the envelope, his shoulders slumped.

'Oh. That *is* disappointing news,' he said.

I looked up, questioning.

'I'm afraid Jenny the orangutan has died.'

I put down my pen, remembering how the little ape had capered about, playing with my handkerchief. Mr Darwin rubbed his forehead.

'That is sad,' I said, my throat tightening, 'what . . .

happened?'

'Oh, it doesn't say. She seemed quite healthy when I saw her last. She was a fascinating study and quite diverting. Still – all is not lost, as they are shipping in a new specimen, a young male by the name of Tommy,' said Mr Darwin, and turned back to his work.

Jenny. All that time Mr Darwin had spent studying her, yet her death was simply inconvenient. The time for moping around was over.

I needed to get bricky.

I clutched the handle of the stinking bucket, gulping deep breaths through my nose, but the smell still made my eyes water. The rain had not let up, but I was glad, although surprised the stink made it through the downpour which soaked my cloak and squelched in my boots and gaiters. I had left the mackerel to turn next to the stove and Mrs Harvey had almost killed me for the stench, but half-rotten mackerel and sardines were now the only foods that would make the dragons take notice.

I rolled my shoulders back, and forced myself to think about Farthing, and how she had been when I had last seen her a week ago. Patrolling the same track back and forth in front of the bars, wearing a path into the soft chalk. All the dragons had taken up some form of repeating movement. Magma and Granite paced a complete circuit of the cave, avoiding Farthing. Basalt scratched repeatedly at the base of his tail and the scales had cracked and fallen away, leaving the skin raw. Sixpence had worn away the scales on one side of her ruff by rubbing the same part over and over against the hot brazier.

At first the dragons had thrived, as our queen had insisted they would. She continued to visit her favourites regularly, which I guessed felt like a fine adventure to her, away from palace life. The mine became more comfortable with each of her visits, the chalk walls whitewashed and set with oil lamps, and rush matting placed underfoot along the tunnels. For nearly half a year the lizards had improved and all grew to the size of Great Danes, but then this new behavioural sickness had started, and it had happened quickly. The Queen refused to accept it, still believing that she had found the answer in her mine enclosure. When Basalt's wound at the base of his tail began to weep, she became angry, blaming the keepers for not attending to him.

That was the last time Queen Victoria had visited. The mines became dull and deserted, with only one keeper, and a guard at the gates.

Her Majesty still corresponded with Mr Darwin and I persuaded him to let me write to her myself, suggesting once again that the dragons be relocated back to the Galapagos on the next survey ship. He wearily agreed. By this time, Mr Darwin had begun courting his cousin, Emma Wedgwood, and was likely to soon be admitted to the esteemed Geological Society. He was working on his *Journal of the Beagle Voyage*, which would be published the following year, and gave regular talks in the top levels of scientific society. He was making the name for himself that he needed to publish his ongoing work, what he called his Big Idea, which seemed to make him awful jittery, in a way I wasn't sure was good for his health. I was curious about this secretive project, and gathered his writings were to do with differences between animals, relating to where they lived, and why some animals survived but others did not. He continued to correspond regularly with Mrs Whitby about her silkworms, and visited other animal breeders. The stuffed Galapagos finches now took pride of place on his desk, and he looked at them often as he frantically scribbled.

More than anything, I feared Farthing and the others would end up as nothing more than a footnote in his studies.

The Queen replied to my letter.

Dear Mr Covington,

In response to your recent correspondence, I am afraid your suggestion remains impossible. I would like to personally commend you on your commitment to their welfare, but these animals will remain safely under my protectorate in perpetuity. I know you will respect my wishes on this matter.

Victoria R.

I wished I had not written. Now I had the Queen's wishes in writing, if I disobeyed . . . it would be treason. I didn't even know what happened to people who committed treason nowadays. In the old days, they'd have their head on a spike on Tower Bridge. I did know it would be a scandal and would affect Mr Darwin's reputation as my master.

Sometimes I was overcome with doubt.

But when I faltered, I thought of Quartz. And Jenny.

CHAPTER FIFTY-SIX

I drew out the key and unlocked the gate set in the bars at the main entrance to the mine, and the damp mossy scent of the cold darkness hit me. I lit the oil lamp that was left by the gate. Mr Darwin had not visited the caves in over a month and had given me free access to the key.

This was down to me, alone.

And tonight was the night for it. The rain had been belting down for days with no sign of stopping, and much of the caves were flooded, which was exactly what I needed.

I felt a surge of hope. The waters were higher than I'd

ever seen them, and it felt like a good sign when I reached the level of the main tunnel and the water lapped at my knees. I waded on to the gate. The dragons were all underwater, floating on their fronts with only their nostrils above the surface. The guard sat on a ledge opposite the barred cavern, smoking a noxious-smelling pipe.

I was relieved to see it was Hallam, the eldest of the team of four guards, all men whose families had worked for the Royals for generations and the Queen had known since childhood. They now worked alone.

I cleared my throat so as not to startle him, but the sound of the water drowned it out. I walked a little closer.

'Evening Mr Hallam, sir,' I said.

The older man did startle, and then slid down from the ledge in the wall that had been cut so the guards would have someplace dry to sit when the caves were wet. He tipped his cap.

'Covington. You really should not be here at this hour. And in this weather. You'll catch your death, boy.'

I shrugged. I liked to release my Bedford accent when talking to the guards alone, and to act my real age. I thanked my lucky stars again that it was old Hallam on duty that night.

'Couldn't sleep, Mr Hallam, sir. You know how afeared I get. I brought the dragons their titbits.'

Hallam nodded, his mutton-chop whiskers seeming to droop a little lower, and a drip from the roof splatted on his cap so he looked up and caught another on his cheek.

'There's no change. They are all in the water, not like they have a lot of choice. The braziers are lit and are above the storm surge, but they don't seem to pay them much notice no more. This flood will soon drain.'

I reached into my cloak, pulled out my hipflask and pretended to take a swig, giving an appreciative shudder. I caught Hallam's envious eye, as I had hoped I would.

'Sorry, Mr Hallam, I should have offered to you first.'

'Ah no, my boy, the Queen gives express orders that no liquor be taken on duty.'

I nodded. 'Well, it's not exactly liquor, Mr Hallam. It's a tonic wine my mam used to swear by to ward off the damp. It might contain a drop of liquor but it ain't the main ingredient, sir. But, can't go against Her Majesty's wishes – 'course not.'

I shrugged and took another faked sip, but before I had slipped it back into my pocket, Hallam huffed a huge cloud of smoke and reached out for the flask.

'I'd say Mother Mary herself wouldn't deny an old man a sip of tonic wine on a night such as this.'

He tipped in a large slug, coughed, and closed his eyes in pleasure.

'It's a very healthful concoction, sir,' I said.

'I would agree with you there, young Covington. A tonic indeed.'

The man took another gulp without removing his clay pipe.

'Oh, that is mighty warming. Your good mother must have . . . do give me the . . .'

The man's words grew thick and trailed off. His pipe dropped from his mouth, and I darted behind him and grabbed him under the armpits as he slumped, lowering him safely on to his ledge. The apothecary had said to measure out the sleeping drops exactly, and I'd calculated that as long as the guard did not take more than two slugs, the tincture couldn't harm him. He'd fallen quickly, as he was slight of build, but the ledge was high enough he would be safe from the flood.

I fetched his pipe and propped it next to him. Then I liberated him of his keys.

CHAPTER FIFTY-SEVEN

The dragons were too big now for me to even imagine hiding them or smuggling them away. Further along the main tunnel of the mine, past the dragons' enclosure, I'd found a drainage pipe. It was big enough for me to crawl through on hands and knees, and led to the main storm drain that must serve this whole area. I knew right away that it was their only chance of escape. I'd removed the grate that covered the drainage pipe and climbed into the main storm drain, which was at least ten foot wide, and a tube not so different from the lava tubes of Narborough – aside from the surging water, the damp and the cold.

So many risks. One chance.

I unlocked the gate and hauled it open, water gushing between the bars. The air was warm inside the dragons' enclosure, the braziers smouldering. Farthing stopped her swimming back and forth along the bars and nudged my hand. She, and the other stronger lizards, understood immediately, as I knew they would. I threw the bucket of rancid fish into the water and Basalt, Magma and Farthing gulped some down. The remaining lizards continued floating, uninterested in the food, but Farthing, Basalt and Magma grabbed pieces in their jaws and nudged at their brothers and sisters with it. The other dragons started to raise their heads above water and take the food. I felt a strange tightness in my chest. What creature cared for its siblings like this? I wished Mr Darwin were here to see it. To see them one last time.

To see me one last time.

Although, if he were here, he'd stop me. Instead, he was safe in his bedchamber – he hadn't woken when I'd left, he wasn't following me.

The movement in the cave was frantic now. The dragons paddled around in a circle and by the dim red light of the braziers, I could not see what the commotion was about. With the water up to my chest and the beat of their powerful tails – they were now the size of young crocodiles – I was feared I'd be dragged under, and could only watch from the wall of the cave where the water was a little more shallow. There was an orchestra of calls, hoots, whines and grunts, then it fell silent. Copper eyes glowed in the light of the brazier, tails batted from side to side. They were miracle creatures, as intelligent as any the world had seen. In their strange language, they had told each other something I would never understand. I fixed a picture of them in my head; my heart aching at my own loss.

Basalt led the way and was out of the gate before I had registered what was happening. The others followed, filing out behind him, butting gently at each other as they disappeared through the gate.

Farthing was last. I followed the others up the tunnel to see where they were going, and it was as I had hoped, they were following the floodwater. Could they smell the freedom of the storm drain, maybe even the open river at the end of it?

My heart pounding, I leant against the wall for a moment. Hallam would be out for a while. I was setting the dragons free into an uncertain world. Well, uncertain was better than certain death.

The Queen had made her wishes very clear. Already, I had committed treason.

I counted the dragons as they passed. Six. I had

somehow known that Farthing would wait, that she would not leave without saying goodbye. But another one was missing.

They were at the very back of the cave. Farthing was circling the last, who was floating with only her nostrils above the water. The smallest. Sixpence. The others had been travelling fast, they had gone, but this changed everything. Sixpence had been burning herself at the brazier, maybe the wound had turned rank, poisoning her blood.

'Go, Farthing, leave her. I will take care of her,' I said.

I grabbed Farthing around the shoulders and tried to shift her, but she growled. She would not leave her sister.

CHAPTER FIFTY-EIGHT

I waded to Sixpence and grasped her around the neck. Her eyes flicked open in recognition, then closed again.

'You can do this. I know you can,' I said.

I skimmed off a handful of the noxious fish I'd thrown in, and held it cupped in my hand to the dragon's nose. Farthing hooted, as if in approval and encouragement, and Sixpence's nostrils flared. Her tongue licked at the mess. She grunted, and hope rose in my chest. I needed to act quickly, not think about how far the others had already gone. I fed her more scooped handfuls of fishy mess, and then grasped her whole body in my arms.

Sixpence didn't struggle. I carried her out of the cave and waded into the floodwater that was now up to my thighs in the mine tunnel. Farthing swam ahead of us, staying close. I made out a faint sound.

Hooting, distant. I wasn't imagining it; I turned my head to hear it with my good ear. I placed Sixpence in the water, and she swam. I waded behind her and Farthing, all the way to the access pipe opening. The hoots were coming from inside.

The water was flowing into the pipe at my knee level, sucking at my legs. Sixpence disappeared into the darkness, half swimming, half walking. Farthing waited, paddling against the flow, watching me.

'I can't come with you,' I said.

She whined.

I stripped off my jacket and pulled off my boots. I needed to get her to the main storm drain and the others.

'Go on then,' I said, 'I'm right behind you.'

I crawled into the access pipe after her on my hands and knees, the water coming up to my elbows and flowing fast.

The other dragons had gathered at the end of the pipe, waiting where the water from the cave tumbled a small waterfall into the huge main storm drain, a churning underground river. As soon as the dragons joined this surge, they would be swept all the way to the Thames. Would they survive it?

I surveyed their strong green-scaled bodies, their copper eyes shining in the dark. They weren't like other animals. They were young dragons. If anything could survive this escape, they could.

The other option was to leave them pacing, trapped, their minds tortured . . . and that was wrong.

I had taken them as eggs, brought them here into danger, and now my only choice was to release them into more danger. Would it be better if I had never taken the eggs in the first place? No. They would have been caught in the solidifying lava, trapped for ever, like flies in amber or one of Mr Darwin's fossils. The dragons huddled together, sniffing at the air, watching the storm surge go by. Waiting.

Waiting for Farthing, who was still by my side.

I crouched, so her head was level with mine. She moved forward and pressed her snout to my forehead and gave the softest hoot, turning into a whine, then a mournful rumbling growl. I held the back of her neck and tried to fix this moment in my mind. The feel of her scales, the heat of her breath, the flash of her eyes.

'Travel safe, Farthing. All of you. Stay bricky,' I said, choked.

The dragons stopped hooting and shuffled, edging

towards the storm drain, sniffing at the air.

'Go,' I said, trying to keep the quiver from my voice. I waved my arm.

Farthing stared up at me.

'Go,' I said again, more forcefully. Farthing hooted, and the first two dragons jumped into the main storm drain and were swept away. Farthing hooted again, and the rest followed.

Her brothers and sisters would quickly be swept away.

'Farthing, you have to go. Now,' I said. I nudged her side and she growled. She didn't want to leave, but how could she care so much for me? When had I come to deserve that? I remembered her mother, that terrifying golden sky beast. Even though she had feared for her eggs, she did not kill me – she allowed me to stay alive, giving me a chance to leave her and her young alone. These animals sensed we were intelligent just as they were, they valued human life.

But Farthing needed to be with her own kind. And they needed her. I pushed her flank, harder with both hands, but she dug her claws into the rock – and then I felt something under her scales, above her shoulder, a hard ridge that had not been there before. I felt again.

Wings.

Farthing was becoming a dragon.

I imagined her golden and magnificent as her mother. In London, caged.

She needed to be somewhere she could fly.

Be bricky.

I waded to where the pipe flowed into the storm drain. A tug at my gaiters, Farthing had me in her jaws, hauling me back from the edge.

I grabbed her snout in my hand and prised the oilcloth of my gaiter free, then summoned all my strength and yelled with everything I had, 'Go, now. You can't stay here. I don't want you!'

The dragon stepped back in surprise, lifting one claw. I had never raised my voice to her.

Farthing whined once, her ruff laid flat. I turned my back on her.

I heard her drop into the surge of the storm drain below. Gone.

CHAPTER FIFTY-NINE

'All of them got away?' said Mr Darwin.

I nodded, and my teeth chattered. I was still shivering, despite the heat of the stove, the blankets wrapped tight around me and the mug of sweet tea in my hands. I had walked most of the night to end up back at Mr Darwin's lodgings just before dawn, although I knew it was selfish to bring him into this. I'd thought to run away, but no further than that. I was so heart-sore, and had nowhere else to go.

'Sorry, sir. I hadn't meant to come back. I left a letter in your study, to the newspaper and the Zoological Society – it says you knew nothing about what I did.'

Darwin rubbed his forehead, his hair sticking up, velvet dressing gown hastily tied over his nightshirt. 'And what is your plan?'

'Plan?'

Yes,' he said impatiently, 'with the lizards under the Queen's protection – and her very specific about her wishes in writing – this could be considered treason.'

I nodded, miserable.

'I don't think you understand, boy.'

'I do, and I am guilty. I will go to the police station now and turn myself in.'

Mr Darwin shook his head violently. 'You certainly will not! The Queen will be furious. Boys have been hanged for less, Covington! She may not show clemency, she is young and prideful, and she does not have a particularly high opinion of me; I will have no sway over her. She could easily send you to the prison hulks, the colonies . . . it doesn't bear thinking . . .' He took a sip of his tea, his hand shaking.

Could I really be hanged for this?

My master was motionless, deep in thought, then sat up straight.

'Did you leave sign of a breakout in the caves?'

I shook my head, not understanding. 'I drugged Hallam and used his key.'

'So, Hallam could have simply fallen asleep leaving

the door unlocked?'

'But Hallam saw me, sir. We spoke, he drank . . .'

Mr Darwin had that familiar light of a new idea in his eyes. 'Did anyone else see you?'

'No – I walked back,' I frowned, as I caught on to his train of thought, '. . . but then Hallam will be blamed—'

'Nonsense. I will see to Hallam's pension myself. He is an old man and should not have been working long hours in the dark and damp, he developed a fever and hallucinated your appearance. It was an accident waiting to happen, this is certainly not his fault.'

Mr Darwin stood and paced, twirling the tasselled cord of his gown. I sat up a little taller myself.

'You will leave on the first passage out of London, Covington. I would suggest . . . Australia or America? I have contacts in both places, I will find you a position.'

He was waiting for a reply, but my head was spinning. I would leave for *good*? I had no family to speak of in England, but there was Mr Darwin. I wrote to Robbins and Davis from the *Beagle*, but they weren't good with their letters so didn't write back often and would both soon be at sea again. I thought of the golden green hills sweeping from restful Sydney harbour, the clear sky and the welcoming people.

'Sydney. I liked . . . Sydney.'

'So did I,' he smiled. 'It is settled then. I will pay for

second class passage under an assumed name. If the police arrive, I will tell them you are in Cambridge fetching a batch of specimens for me.'

My throat filled. I hadn't imagined this, or anything like this.

'But I can't, I will not – your reputation, your important studies, your book. It is too much risk to you, sir.'

When Mr Darwin fixed me with those clear eyes, I saw he was decided.

'It is a risk I choose to take,' he said, and his voice dropped. 'The lizards were going to die there, Covington, eventually. With the Queen's involvement, I could see no way to prevent it. But you . . . you set them free, so I will set you free. I will not argue on this, my boy, it is decided.'

It was my turn to nod. I thumbed hot tears from the corners of my eyes and edged closer to the fire.

'Farthing wouldn't leave. I had to shout at her, to make her go,' I mumbled. Mr Darwin's eyebrows rose in the middle as he shook out a clean handkerchief and handed it to me.

'That must have been very hard, dear boy,' he said, and paused, 'but you did what was best, let them take their own chances. It was brave. Now – you have your own escape to think on.'

Australia.

I sniffed. 'I'll never be able to thank you, sir,' I said.

Mr Darwin poured more tea.

'Well, in that case, we are in the same boat. So to speak.'

My good master clapped my shoulder, and then squeezed it hard, his hand warm through my damp clothes.

I saw his own eyes were wet and shining.

The memory came to me, and I am sure it came to him, of the pitching waves. Of a boy and a man lost at sea, and a rope held tight by two pairs of hands.

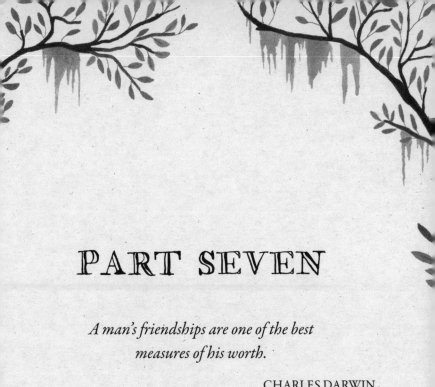

PART SEVEN

*A man's friendships are one of the best
measures of his worth.*

CHARLES DARWIN

CHAPTER SIXTY

Twenty-five years later

The dark mound of Narborough Island eased closer, silhouetted against the hot blue sky. Eleven-year-old Emmeline Covington's heart danced in her chest as she gripped the rails of the rowboat. She was really *here*. The Enchanted Isles, the setting of all her pa's most fantastical stories. When Pa promised he'd bring her here one day, she'd thought that was one of his stories too.

It had only been ten days since they left Lima in Peru, but the voyage from Australia had been six weeks, so it was strange that this short trip by rowboat to the island, seemed to be taking longest. Pa's stories of his adventures on this Galapagos island had been the backdrop of Emmie's imagination for her whole life, as familiar as the red Australian dust that usually clung to her boots. Until now. Now her boots were salt-stained and bleached by the sun, and she was going to find out how much of Pa's stories were built of truth, and how much make-believe filled the gaps.

'At least the sea is a little calmer than the first time I visited,' said Pa, taking a swig from the water flask and passing it to her, 'a perfect Greenish Blue.'

Pa was right. There was barely a wave, and the boat rocked gently with the rowing of the men.

'What colour was the sea during the shipwreck storm with Mr Darwin?' asked Emmie.

'Well, I could barely tell the colour . . . since so much of it was in my eyes,' a smile was in his voice, 'but I suppose it was an angry Greenish Grey, with a foam of Skimmed-milk White.'

Pa had taught Emmie the special colour descriptions that Mr Darwin used from Werner's book for as long as she could remember. She liked the animal descriptions that went with each colour the best.

'Ahh . . . like the White of the Human Eye,' she said, smiling, her own eyes clinging to the peak of the island.

'Sounds about right!' said Pa with a low laugh. 'Certainly saw the whites of my eyes that day.'

'And Mr Darwin's!' she said.

'Definitely Mr Darwin's. He was never a good sailor at the best of times.'

At last they hit the shore of Narborough Island. One of the burly sailors swung Emmie down, out of the rowboat on to the jagged rocks, and she wobbled with the strangeness of being on dry land. Her mind wobbled too, with the oddity of the place. Pa had said the Galapagos would be completely different to anything she had seen, but Emmie still hadn't been prepared. It was so . . . dark and bare. The grey rocks, the black lava plains, the peak of the volcano, no longer smoking. There were no 'imps of darkness' lizards that Pa had told her about, but she did catch sight of a few Sally Lightfoot crabs, scuttling between rocks. She'd have to take a closer look later. There were no sea lions either, which was a shame as Farthing's leap on to the fighting sea lion's head was one of her favourite stories. But at least there were the white birds with the bright blue feet. Blue-footed boobies. She had always laughed at the name and wondered if Pa had made it up, but now saw how it suited them.

Emmie approached one of the birds for a closer look,

and it didn't move. She waved at it. It looked away. She took out her tin whistle from her pocket. She'd never taken to the fiddle like Pa and her sister, or piano like Mama and her brothers.

She played a jolly tune. The bird opened its black beak wide, as if yawning. She laughed and turned to Pa. 'I don't think he likes my music.'

Pa grinned. 'It was the same when I was here as a boy, the animals don't know humans, so they haven't learnt to be cautious . . . although I'm sure he'll soon learn to be afraid of that whistle.'

Emmie tried to glare at her pa, and failed.

The sun pounded hot on the crown of the wide-brimmed straw hat they'd bought to replace her bonnet at the market in Lima. Much to her delight, Pa had also purchased her boy's clothing in sturdy beige linen, stout boots and canvas gaiters, so she looked like a smaller version of him. It was very strange to wear trousers – so free. She wasn't sure what Mama would have thought. Pa called it 'expedition clothing', essential for where they were going. She thought of Mama now, still unable to believe she had allowed her go. Emmie was the second youngest of eight children, her oldest brothers, Syms Junior and Charles, were both grown up and Syms had been married last year; they were running the Post Office while Pa was gone. Her elder sister, Bess, would help Mama, when she wasn't out courting with the butcher's son and playing her fiddle. Eddie, Alf and Phillip would be eating all the bread and butter as quick as Mama could bake and churn it, but they worked hard on the homestead and Phillip had promised to read to her youngest brother, Walter, while she was away.

Emmie wouldn't be missed, not really. She'd always been a bit different to the others, with her rock collection, dusty skirts and her tin whistle. Pa was the person she spent most time with. The family were surprised when he told them his plans, but not so much that he was only taking one of them, and it would be Emmie.

She looked at Pa now. He was gazing up at the volcano through the eyeglass.

'I expect you'll tell me you are searching for dragons,' she said. Usually he would have taken this opportunity to tell her every detail about the golden fire-breathing dragon, who had thrown him into the sea and hunted him, about how Farthing had saved him, and then turned out to be a baby dragon herself. Emmie would shake her head and tut, because she was too old for his stories, and Pa would laugh. But today Pa said nothing.

Emmie followed his gaze, but there was nothing to see. She was more interested in the ground, watching for lizards of green.

'Do you think Darwin's Dragons are really here, Pa?'

Pa put his arm around Emmie shoulders and gave her a squeeze.

CHAPTER SIXTY-ONE

Emmie pulled the sheets and blankets up to her chin, the slope of the tent canvas was rippling ever so slightly above her in the gentle evening breeze. They'd only had time to explore a little before nightfall, when the two sailors Pa had employed were setting up the camp. Emmie had passed the dead chimney-like fumaroles, and miles of black sandy soil dotted with cactuses, she'd even tried the famous prickly pear; which wasn't quite as delicious when a person wasn't marooned and dying of thirst. Her camp bed was set behind a cotton curtain and was as comfortable as she could ask for. Pa's section of the tent had a small desk and a lamp.

She watched his silhouette. Her eyes stung with tiredness, but her mind raced.

'Get some sleep now, Emmie,' said Pa, although she hadn't made a sound. He turned down the lamp, 'we'll be up at daybreak.'

'Play for me?' she said.

Pa sighed, but fetched his fiddle all the same, and then the swooping notes of the lullaby he'd written for her as a baby filled her ears and switched off her mind. Her eyes instantly grew heavy...

The cream canvas slanting above her suddenly ballooned inwards, with a ripping sound. Pa's fiddle screeched a jarring note and Emmie gasped and covered her head, thinking something had fallen on them, or the whole tent was coming down.

'Pa?' She sprung up in bed, as the canvas billowed back out again. 'Pa! What was that?' she said, swinging her legs over the side of the bed, staring up at the canvas, blinking.

'Stay where you are, Emmie, don't move,' he hissed.

She hugged herself, teeth clenched tight. It must have been a huge gust of wind? Just out of nowhere? But the canvas was now still, it made no sense. Unless . . . it had been something above, passing overhead. But it would have to have been . . . huge.

Pa and one of the other men spoke in hushed tones at

the entrance of the tent, and then he came back in and crouched by her bed. He tucked in the covers and kissed her forehead.

'What was it?'

'I don't know for certain. But it's gone now. Get some rest.' He looked down at her, but his eyes were far away, and they didn't seem afraid. They shone in the yellow light of the oil lamp.

Suddenly Emmie wondered if it was possible Pa had always told her the truth. About everything. That *none* of it was make-believe. No, that was impossible.

But whatever made the tent move like that, hadn't been an albatross, or a blue-footed booby, or a flamingo, or any of the other Galapagos animals he'd told her about.

There was only one thing in the air that big.

And it wasn't . . . real.

CHAPTER SIXTY-TWO

Emmie was surprised when the sailors left early the next morning. The men said they would fish in the waters around this and the other Galapagos islands, and come back the next day. She hadn't actually thought that her and Pa would be left on the island, alone. She skipped to keep up with Pa's fast pace, as he cut a straight line towards the centre of the island. He was quiet, his eyes pinned to the volcano.

Pa had been a bit odd this morning, when she'd asked again about what could have made the canvas billow out that way, he'd just replied that he didn't know. Every half an hour he stopped to scan the sky with his eyeglass, and on more than one occasion she saw him reading the old crumpled letter from Mr Darwin that he always kept in his breast pocket. It was the one thing he'd always kept secret.

The sun rose in the sky and passed overhead, and finally Pa stopped and scanned the entire sky. Then he flicked back his hat and used his neckerchief to wipe the sweat from his brow.

'It's like I can feel them,' he said, as if to himself.

'The lizards? Farthing?' asked Emmie.

He didn't reply.

They finally stopped to eat, resting their backs against a fumarole which rose like a black jagged chimney to Emmie's waist.

She pointed at a small bird, pecking at a yellow flower on one of the prickly pear cactuses.

'Pa! Isn't that one of Mr Darwin's finches? The one with the big beak that you drew for him?'

'Hmm yes. The common cactus finch.'

Emmie frowned. She'd expected Pa to tell her again about the day he found it, explain the bird had a different beak because it ate different food, and that the birds with the right beaks would breed to produce more birds the same. He'd quote Mr Darwin's remarkable book, *On the Origin of Species*, that had arrived in the post last year, which had a whole shelf to itself in the parlour back home, and Emmie wouldn't interrupt, even though she might have heard this exact part many times before. Emmie suddenly realized that Pa must have started planning this trip just after he received the book everyone was making so much fuss about back in England. The Big Idea Mr Darwin had worked on for so long had made Pa's former master such a famous man. Pa said Mr Darwin was scared of what people might think of his theory; he joked that he knew the feeling, because his master hadn't thought much of his own ideas . . . about dragons.

But Pa was quiet now, chewing slowly, thoughtful. Emmie bolted the cold potatoes, fish and prickly pear, washed it down with water, then slid her tin whistle out of the pocket in her breeches. She played a lively jig Pa had taught her, one from when he was fiddler on the *Beagle*.

High fluting notes flew across the empty plain before them, with no echo, snatched by the clear air. She played on, blending one tune into the next, lost in the music, until her father sprung to his feet with a gasp.

The whistle dropped from Emmie's mouth.

'What is—' She stood and clutched Pa's arm.

A black silhouette above the peak of the volcano. Bat-like wings, powerful body, legs hanging below. It flew at such speed, it grew bigger by the second, and although Pa pressed Emmie to get down, she grabbed him, and instead he put his arm around her shoulder, and she felt him tremble. They both raised their chins to stare.

They were powerless, tiny; there was nothing to be done, nowhere to hide, because it was flapping directly towards them.

A soaring giant of glinting gold.

A dragon.

CHAPTER SIXTY-THREE

The dragon swooped low, and Emmie's body told her to crouch and cover her head, but instead she froze, Pa's strong arm tight around her. She gaped upwards at its pale belly and the mighty claws, as it swept overhead, casting them in its long shadow. The wind from its enormous wings battered their upturned faces, whisking up dust. It raced past, then soared upwards and around, banking back.

It hovered between them and the volcano, wings spread wide, the bright sky shining through their thin leather. With the sun darting off its scales, the dragon looked like something owned by the Gods of Olympus in the Greek myths Mama used to read to her, and she quaked and clung to Pa.

The dragon dropped from the sky like a stone, only at the last moment flapping its wings in one final eye-watering blast, and landing gracefully on all four of its powerful legs.

It was now only fifty or so steps away from Emmie and Pa. A hillock of gold.

Pa released his hold around her shoulders and turned. 'Stay here,' he whispered.

She grabbed his hand to stop him, unable to tear her eyes from the dragon's head, wider at the top and crested by two deep bronze spiralling horns. Its huge golden eyes flashed, its snout tapered to dark nostrils. Did the fire come from those or its mouth? Emmie couldn't remember what Pa had told her.

Pa eased his hand from hers. She wanted to hold on to him, but didn't dare make a fuss, didn't dare attract its attention, which was all on Pa. Was this the mother dragon? It certainly looked exactly how her father had described her.

Emmie swallowed as Pa removed his rifle and placed it on the ground, followed by his knapsack and finally his hat. He had nothing but the clothes he was wearing.

Pa put out both of his hands, palms up in front of him, and slowly walked towards the dragon.

How to describe its size? Bigger than four stage-coaches all squashed together, but much longer with its tail as well. Its wings were now folded against its body. Pa stopped only a yard or so in front of it and Emmie's heart pounded in her throat. The dragon ducked its head, so its eyes were on a level with her father's, except its head was bigger than Pa's whole body and its eye bigger than Pa's head. She gasped with fear for him and covered her mouth to stop herself crying out. It blinked, and then made the most curious sound she had ever heard.

Something like a rumble that vibrated in the base of her belly, but then turned more like the hoot of an owl.

And her father . . . laughed.

The dragon raised a crest of scales behind its horns in a waving motion, and Emmie noticed one was missing.

She'd once asked Pa how he could tell Darwin's Dragons apart, when they all grew to the same size. He said Farthing always had a scale missing on the ruff at her neck.

Pa had told her – he had told Mr Darwin and Ma too – that the miraculous golden eggs were the dragon's eggs, that the green lizards Queen Victoria had loved would grow into giant golden beasts . . .

When he was a boy only a little older than she was now, he'd set them free.

All this time. All this time, and no one had believed him.

But Pa's stories were the truth.

And now Emmie's amazing Pa was beside Farthing – Farthing the dragon – and his hand was on the side of her muzzle, and he was talking to her, although Emmie could not hear what he said.

Her heart danced a jig in her throat, but she could not stop grinning, as she watched Farthing gently butt her nose against Pa's chest and hoot again.

She walked towards them, her fear buried under her fascination.

Emmie gripped Pa's hand tight, as the dragon swung her head back and arched to look down at her. Farthing's eyes were impossibly beautiful, no longer copper as a new farthing, but fiery rippling gold, with a deep slit of darkness at the centre. The dragon sniffed and she was so giant, Emmie felt the suction on her clothing. Then Farthing released a gentle hoot, almost a whine, lowered her head and tilted it to one side.

'Stay bricky. She can tell who you are,' said Pa.

Emmie shrugged out of his grip, and when she reached up, fingers trembling, the dragon tilted her head further down to meet her. Farthing's ruff rippled as Emmie's hand rested beneath her eye. Her scales were warm and smooth, each one the size of her hand.

Emmie was touching a dragon. This was Pa's Farthing, all grown up.

CHAPTER SIXTY-FOUR

Emmie felt tears prickle her eyes, and when Farthing huffed and made that rumbling hooting sound, the sob in her throat turned into a laugh.

'Pa told me all about you, Farthing. You're . . .' she faltered, 'you've . . . grown.'

Pa chuckled, and stroked Farthing's scales next to Emmie's hand.

Then Farthing raised her head and they both stepped back. She reared up on her hind legs and unfurled her wings. With a few almighty flaps, she took flight and hovered in the air above them, and then she was soaring, circling, releasing joyful hoots so loud they vibrated through the ground and up Emmie's legs.

'She's so happy to see you,' said Emmie.

Pa squeezed her hand tight. 'All these years . . . and really she hasn't changed at all.'

Farthing swept down towards them again, but this time her claws stretched out, tensing, and she hovered briefly above their heads. She circled and dived, flexing her front claws again.

'What is she doing?' Emmie asked Pa.

'Wait here,' he said, 'and stay bricky.'

Emmie didn't like the sound of that but didn't have time to argue. Pa ran back to the fumarole and hopped up on to the rim of it, catching his balance. She stared at him in disbelief, as he raised both his arms and waved up at Farthing, who was now circling them.

The next time the dragon swept down, she came straight as an arrow, and Pa stood upright, both his hands in the air.

He couldn't be planning to . . .

'Pa!'

Farthing swerved sideways and snatched him up, her giant claws wrapped around his middle. Emmie couldn't take it in, Pa had lost his mind! She ran after them, in the dragon's shadow.

'No fear . . . I trust her with my . . . life . . .' Pa's voice whipped away as he was swept into the sky. He waved, his other arm clutching a claw as long as his forearm.

Emmie covered her mouth, as the dragon – Farthing – swept her own pa up and over the ocean, and then circled back towards her. She took her eyes from them just long enough to find the eyeglass on top of Pa's knapsack. She stared through it as they passed overhead, and Pa's face came into focus, grinning like one of the town boys riding a go-cart down the hill. Beyond Farthing, in the distant blue, she caught another flash of gold.

Emmeline Covington counted one, two . . . seven more dragons, weaving and wheeling a glittering trail across the sky.

PEOPLE AND PLACES IN DARWIN'S DRAGONS

THE PEOPLE

Syms Covington

In this story, Syms Covington (Syms was short for Simon) is a fictional character, based on a real person. Historians don't know for sure when the real Syms was born, and it is likely he was a little older than he is in my story. But in the 1830s, boys as young as eight years old could sign on to a ship as cabin boy. Syms really did start as cabin boy and ship's fiddler on HMS *Beagle*, and was promoted to Charles Darwin's assistant around two years into the voyage. Syms returned with Darwin to London, and they worked together until he moved to Australia. They continued to write to each other, and although the writing is formal, as it was in Victorian times, it seems to me they had definitely become friends. Syms wrote a very brief journal during the *Beagle* voyage, but there was a gap in it during the journey around the Galapagos Islands, which I jumped upon. I had just the adventure to fill those pages.

Charles Darwin

Charles Darwin was only twenty-two when he set sail on the *Beagle*, so in this story he would be a young man of twenty-six, nothing like the bushy-bearded grandpa in the photos we are used to seeing. One of my favourite things about Darwin is that he ended up doing something very different with his life than was planned for him. He was supposed to be a doctor, but didn't like blood; then was supposed to be a vicar, but wasn't interested in that either, and hated exams. Darwin was full of curiosity and wonder, and from a very young age, loved collecting animals. It was when he started following his dreams that wonderful things happened.

In Charles Darwin's time, most people in Europe and America believed what the Bible told them was fact – that God created the world in six days. But during his voyage on the *Beagle*, Darwin began to observe nature very closely and question everything he'd been taught. He found evidence that living things could naturally change over very long periods of time . . . which eventually led to his groundbreaking theory of evolution. Darwin knew that his ideas would shock people, and would anger and upset many, but today, scientists accept that evolution is a fact. Charles Darwin changed history, and it all started with the strange and wonderful things he saw during his voyage on the *Beagle*, and especially in the Galapagos Islands.

Queen Victoria

In June 1837, the eighteen-year-old Victoria became Queen. She is another historical person we mostly associate with being an older lady, dressed in black and looking rather grim. But in my book she is lively and curious, still a teenager, just finding her way as the new Queen of England. Queen Victoria had a very strict, controlled upbringing called The Kensington System, where she wasn't ever allowed to be alone, had to sleep in her mother's bedroom, was kept away from other children, never allowed sweet foods and barely ever left the palace. I imagine she would have been delighted with her new freedom when she became Queen of England, able to boss everyone else around for a change, and ready for an adventure that took her outside the prison-like palace. Victoria really did love animals and definitely met Jenny the orangutan.

Mary Anne Whitby

In Darwin's time, there were not many opportunities for women to work in Science, but Mary Anne Whitby and Darwin wrote letters to each other later in his life. She was a silkworm breeder, and her experiments helped Darwin develop his theory of natural selection.

Emmeline Covington

Emmeline really was Syms Covington's youngest daughter. Very little is known about her, so I have given her a fully-fictional adventure.

The officers and sailors

Captain Fitzroy commanded the *Beagle*, and all sailors in this book – the marine Robbins, the ship's surgeon Bynoe, the cook and the ship's boy – were on the *Beagle*'s papers; real members of crew.

THE PLACES

The Galapagos Islands

The Galapagos Islands are an archipelago of volcanic islands situated across the equator in the Pacific Ocean. They are part of Ecuador in South America, and are now a national park and marine reserve. Many animals that live there are not found anywhere else in the world, so are very rare.

Narborough Island is a real place, now known as Fernandina Island. It is the second largest island of the Galapagos, but Darwin never went there. Fernandina does have an active shield volcano, which erupted ten years before my story is set, plus lava tube tunnels. It has no source of fresh water and nobody lives there permanently, even now. The Galapagos animals Syms encounters are also all real, and it is reasonable to imagine they could have lived on Fernandina at the time. Including the dragons, of course!

The *Beagle*

The *Beagle* was a brig – a wooden ship, powered by sails, and was considered to be the fifth-fastest vessel in England at the time. But it was small, at around twenty-eight metres long, which is only the length of two double-decker buses! Between sixty and seventy-three crew were onboard the *Beagle*, so living conditions were very cramped. Darwin slept in the tiny poop cabin, in a hammock he strung up every evening over the table where the officers read their charts.

Under the orders of Captain Fitzroy, the *Beagle* had been fitted with a new, raised deck which helped keep it stable in the water. He did this as this type of ship had such a bad habit of sinking – they were known as 'coffin brigs'. I am guessing they probably didn't tell Charles Darwin that!

It may seem strange to name a ship after a breed of dog, but naming ships after animals is common in the British Royal Navy. Some of my favourite navy ship names are HMS *Greyhound*, HMS *Bulldog*, HMS *Bat*, HMS *Beaver*, HMS *Ferret* and HMS *Peacock*!

AN INTERVIEW WITH
LINDSAY GALVIN

How did you come up with the idea to combine dragons with Charles Darwin's famous voyage?

This planet was once home to the magnificent dinosaurs, so why not dragons?

The plan for this story was about real-world dragons, animals that felt like they could exist and weren't fantastical. My publishers asked me to add a small historical part, and I immediately thought of Darwin's famous voyage, as I already knew a bit about it from teaching the evolution topic to year six. I started to research the voyage of the *Beagle*, and discovered that Darwin promoted the cabin boy and ship's fiddler, Syms Covington, to be his personal servant, and to assist on expeditions and with collecting specimens. When I wrote Syms' part of the story, it just felt right somehow; *Darwin's Dragons* had hatched!

This is your first historical novel. Did that make it more difficult to write?

I am fascinated by the past and read a lot of historical books for adults and children, but never thought I could write one myself. It was hard enough getting a story right without having to research a different time as well! So I was surprised when the voice of Syms flowed out quite easily. No matter what the story is, for me, the characters come first. It was only once I had written the first draft and my characters and plot were in place, that I began researching to get the historical details right. That took me months! But I didn't mind as I loved learning more about this era. During the 1800s the steam train, electric lighting, matches, bicycles, stamps and so much more, were all invented. Louis Pasteur came up with his germ theory, Michael Faraday discovered the connection between electricity and magnetism and Mary Anning was digging up dinosaur bones on the west coast of England. It seemed a perfect time to discover dragons.

How did you research the story?

It was huge fun. I read lots of books and researched on the internet as I wrote. Then I visited the Natural History Museum, and took a tour behind the scenes where I saw the actual specimens collected on the *Beagle*. I went to Downe House, where Darwin lived for most of his life, and stood in Darwin's study, then I spoke to some amazing experts who described Darwin's life after the *Beagle*. I visited Chislehurst Caves and some caves in Portugal, to inspire the underground scenes. I watched David Attenborough's wondrous *Galapagos* TV series many times. And I read Charles Darwin's *The Voyage of the Beagle*. I observed, and gently handled, lizards at a reptile sanctuary, to watch their behaviour and movement, and visited Marwell Zoo and London Zoo.

How much of the story is true?

I've tried to keep it as accurate as possible – the equipment, the boat and the settings. Everything outside of Darwin's interactions with Syms, the lizards and Queen Victoria actually happened.

I also added in historical facts I discovered in my research. Darwin really was very seasick and hated the sight of blood, which stopped him becoming a doctor. He did have a home-made eyeglass, like the one in this story, I saw it on display at his home, Downe House. And he really did ride a giant Galapagos tortoise.

Syms Covington and Farthing have a very special bond. Did you have any pets growing up?

My first pet, at age nine, was Chestnut the hamster, who lived to nearly four years old – over one hundred in hamster years! Then we had Baggins, the African grey parrot, who used to soak his seeds and titbits in water and throw them at me from his cage, and shout my name in my dad's voice. Now I have my two cats, brother and sister, Buster and Flinty, who fill my house with fluff and cuddles, fight over who can leave the most fur on my desk chair and tell miaowing tales on each other.

Tell us about the dragons . . .

My instinct is always to try to make things as believable as I can, with lots of science involved. The world is so full of weird and wonderful creatures so I took all my inspiration from nature and started by researching those flying prehistoric giants, the pterosaurs, and studying the behaviour of other dinosaurs. I gave my dragons a very strange life cycle, stolen from creatures like frogs and butterflies, which go through a metamorphosis – the features of their body changing as they grow. I combined this with the ability to survive over very long periods, like the Greenland shark, which can live to 500 years old.

I hope that I have made breathing fire seem real. Because, why not? Animals have evolved many defences that seem magical; from stings and bites, spitting venom and acid, to electrocution. All fire needs is a spark, fuel and oxygen. I invented a dragon with sharp plates in the back of its throat, that could grind together to make a terrible scream, and friction that produces a spark. Then I gave my dragon a special chamber above its stomach, to store flammable gases released by digestion, which would act as fuel. The spark meets the fuel and hits the oxygen in the air . . . let there be fire!

How does this story, based 185 years ago on Darwin's voyage on the **Beagle**, *relate to what is happening in the world today?*

Syms Covington discovered a frightening fact; that most people refuse to believe what they haven't seen with their own eyes. Today we have a similar situation with the slow but steady differences we are noticing due to climate change. A threat much more frightening than any dragon.

Science often tells us things we don't want to hear. The Victorians didn't want to believe in evolution; to hear that humans descended from apes. The Bible had taught them humans were different and better than other animals. So, Charles Darwin waited twenty-three years before publishing his groundbreaking book *On the Origin of Species*, because he didn't want to cause trouble and upset his family and friends. Now his findings provide the basis of nearly all the biology we study.

There are scientists in the same position as Darwin was, right now, but this time their findings are very urgent. It's taken activists, like the brilliant sixteen-year-old, Greta Thunberg, to show us that we must listen to scientists, even if it is hard to hear what they tell us. Darwin had time to spare. We do not. It might not be affecting most of our lives yet, but climate change is a fact, and every one of us can do something about it.

Young people, like you, are willing to believe what they cannot see, and are as fiercely protective of our planet as a dragon over her eggs. It is you who will stop us burning. Thank you.

CHARLES DARWIN TIMELINE

1809 12th February. Charles Darwin was born in Shrewsbury, a small village in England. His father was a doctor and his mother the daughter of a famous china factory owner, and they lived in a large house.

As a small child, he spent most of his time outside and collected birds' eggs (only one from each nest) and pebbles. He also loved to read.

1817 Darwin's mother died. His three older sisters and older brother helped looked after him and his younger sister.

1818 Darwin was sent away to boarding school, age nine. He hated being away from home and wasn't a good student – he couldn't remember all the things he was supposed to. But he loved science and made a chemistry lab in a tool shed in his garden at home! His friends nicknamed him 'Gas'.

1825 Darwin was not doing well at school, so was sent to Edinburgh University medical school with his older brother, who was becoming a doctor. Darwin hated watching operations and finally confessed to his father, a year later, that he didn't want to be a doctor.

1828 Darwin was sent to Cambridge to train to be a vicar, as many vicars studied nature as a hobby. He didn't enjoy studying and spent most of his time outside again, collecting beetles.

1831   Darwin was given the chance to be a 'gentleman companion' and naturalist (someone who studied nature) on Captain Fitzroy's round-the-world voyage on the *Beagle,* which would be away for at least two years.

On 27th December the *Beagle* left Plymouth.

1832   January. The *Beagle* reached Cape Verde, north of the equator off Africa. Darwin started reading about geology and the ideas of a geologist called Charles Lyell, who believed the earth had formed over a long period of time. He decided to collect specimens, explore and ask questions, to investigate this idea.

September. Darwin discovered fossils off the coast of Argentina.

1832–35   Darwin visited Patagonia, Rio de Janeiro, Uruguay, Chile and climbed the Andes mountains, all the while collecting specimens, observing the mountains and rocks, and witnessing an earthquake.

1835   15th September. The *Beagle* arrived at the Galapagos Islands. Darwin collected the famous Galapagos finches and many other unusual animals.

1836   October. After visiting Tahiti, New Zealand, Australia and South Africa, the *Beagle* returned to England.

1837   Darwin pursued his career as a scientist. He turned his *Beagle* diary into a book and had the help of experts to identify the specimens he collected.

1838 Darwin visited Jenny the orangutan at London Zoo. By October, he was developing a theory about how animals can change over generations – as all animals of a species are unique, some are better-adapted to survive than others. Those are the animals that have offspring of their own, passing on these adaptations to the next generation . . . this would end up being called 'natural selection'. He kept his work secret, so as not to upset people.

1839 29ᵗʰ January. Darwin married his cousin, Emma Wedgwood, and moved to the country to have a family, living at Downe House in Kent.

Darwin published his *Journal of Researches*, based on his *Beagle* diary.

1858 By now, Darwin had a large family and was a very relaxed and fun father, compared to most Victorian dads. He even made a slide for his children on the stairs! Sadly, three of his ten children died – this was much more common in those days, before antibiotics and other medicines had been invented.

Darwin received a letter from Alfred Russell Wallace, who lived in Malaysia, showing he had the same ideas about natural selection. Darwin decided to reveal his theory, but wanted to be fair to Wallace, so both theories were read aloud at a scientific meeting when neither scientist was there. Darwin had written his notes in 1844 so he was considered the man to discover evolution.

1859   *On the Origin of Species by Means of Natural Selection* was published. It is still considered one of the most important science books ever written. There was uproar in England and everyone argued about the book, but as time passed, most scientists began to accept Darwin's ideas.

1871   *The Descent of Man* was published. Darwin wrote that human beings were not descended from Adam and Eve, but were part of the animal kingdom and evolved like any other species. People were outraged and cartoons were drawn of Darwin as a hairy monkey!

1881   Darwin published his last book about earthworms. He never wanted to be famous and continued to be a scientist; questioning, observing and writing, even when very ill.

1882   Darwin died aged 73.

READING LIST

About Charles Darwin

The Beagle with Charles Darwin Fiona MacDonald and Mark Bergin (Book House, 2015)

Charles Darwin's On the Origin of Species Sabina Radeva (Puffin, 2019)

Darwin: The Man, His Great Voyage, and His Theory of Evolution John van Whye (André Deutsch, 2018)

What Mr Darwin Saw Mick Manning and Brita Granström (Frances Lincoln Children's Books, 2009)

Who Was Charles Darwin? Deborah Hopkinson (Penguin, 2005)

About Queen Victoria

My Name is Victoria, Lucy Worsley (Bloomsbury Children's Books, 2017)

V&A Introduces: Queen Victoria (Puffin, 2019)

ACKNOWLEDGEMENTS

With heartfelt thanks to:

My agent, Laura Williams. You are my trusted ally through good times and bad, my honest guide and enthusiastic supporter. You trust my wild ideas and rein me in just the right amount. I wouldn't want to be doing this without you.

My editor, Rachel Leyshon. You found a historical middle-grade heart to me that I never knew I had, and this story wouldn't exist without our creative collaboration on the initial ideas. I truly appreciate you giving me the space to explore, and the opportunity to write something completely different. I'm so happy I made you cry!

My publisher, Barry Cunningham. You gave me the choice of which way to go with this book and the confidence to follow the route the story had naturally taken. It made the process a true pleasure. The final flight is for you.

Elinor for launching this voyage around the world on 27th December, just like the *Beagle*. Jazz, Esther, Kesia and all the brilliant Chicken House coop for your detailed input, creativity and kindness.

The team who worked on the stunning cover. It's better than anything I could have imagined due to the vision of Rachel Hickman, the design skill of Steve

Wells, and the artwork of Gordy Wright. Flaps and maps! I am so delighted.

Darwin's Dragons arrived during a turbulent time. Just after I sold this book, I became seriously ill with an anxiety disorder. I spent months out of myself, and out of the world. I didn't write again until I was ready, and then this story was kind to me and came easily. So the following people also deserve special thanks for carrying me through that time and having faith when I didn't. Mostly for being quietly there.

All my friends, old and new, online and in person. My uni crew, there for each other for the last twenty-one years through anything life throws us, a huge support. My work friends and colleagues who cheer me on, and the management team who were so kind and understanding as I transitioned back into teaching. The home gang, who've swept me up when I needed it. To Stuart White, for your trust and empathy, and the #writementor community – because helping other people has really helped me. To the many writing friends who are there for me, but a special mention for Sarah Harris and Giles Paley-Phillips and all the help, patience and endless chats.

Jo Hogan. My first port of call, in a storm or otherwise. Not many people have read this book, but you have, and as usual saw to the heart of it. I've come to value your judgement alongside my own. Thanks for being there for me when you can't have had anything else to give. My true, dear friend.

My Sally. This time round it hasn't been all about the fun. You've shared your understanding and calm during dark times. Just knowing you are there makes me feel better, love. Not forgetting Paul, Elly and Isla and the menagerie – my dear 'framily'.

All of my extended family. Special thanks to the Galvin clan for shouting far and wide.

To my gem of a mother-in-law Pam – for the chats, childcare and many kindnesses. Pete, Anne, Millie, Juliet, Ray, Lottie and Lucy who are always there when we need you. RIP to our wonderful Aunty Fran, gone too soon. I strive to enjoy life as much as you did.

My mum, the original keeper of dragons, you still pick me up now with your love and kindness, as you always have. Dad, for making me smile when I didn't know I could, recognize the pond scene and the capsize drill? Rob and Jo, for being my retreat when I descend without warning. Syms and Farthing's bond is for you. Kathryn, little Emmie reminds me of you and Farthing is your Starlite, you are simply the best sister from glass eyes to lost keys and way beyond.

My cats Buster and Flinty. My sister's dogs Erynn, Phoebe and Martha. For all the many therapy cuddles,

I've appreciated the fur babies more this year than ever before. Farthing contains a little of all of you. Yes I'm also acknowledging pets, well done for reading this far!

My older son Ed, for openly talking about everything, you're instinctively understanding and always make me laugh. My younger son, Oscar, for all the story sharing, for letting me into your awesome imagination, and your natural kindness. I'm so blessed to have you both.

Bill. You do so much for me I don't know where to start. Sharing this life with you makes it shine. You are the master of everyday acts of love. I promise to try to make better coffee.

RIP Theresa Honeyands.

My beloved Nanna died peacefully aged 94 just as I was about to hand in my final edit on this story. I hit my deadline for her, remembering how she always found peace and joy in making things. I love and miss her. I think she'd have liked this story.